RY

J. D. IRWIN

Catnip

CATNIP BOOKS
Published by Catnip Publishing Ltd
Quality Court, off Chancery Lane
London WC2A 1HR

This edition first published 2013
1 3 5 7 9 10 8 6 4 2

Cover illustration by Andy Parker
Cover design by Mandy Norman

A CIP catalogue record for this book is available from the
British Library.

ISBN 978-1-84647-166-7

Printed and bound by CPI Group (UK) Ltd, Croydon, CR0 4YY

www.catnippublishing.co.uk

FOR JAMIE

PROLOGUE

THE YOUNG WOMAN SUDDENLY STIRRED from her sleep. A relic was being touched . . . touched by a human hand. Her eyes opened and she sat up.

'Which relic?' she whispered to herself. She fumbled in the early morning light for a glass ball. It glowed a faint orange, but after a few seconds she shook her head impatiently then repeated, '*Which* relic?'

The sphere's glow faded. Getting to her feet, she began to pace around the room. Why couldn't she recognise the relic? Was it too far away? She should be able to tell *anything* within the territories . . .

The woman stopped dead and her eyes widened. She cupped the sphere in both hands and held it up to her face.

'I need to see the king,' she whispered, and the glass glowed deep red.

CHAPTER ONE

EDWIN SPENCER HAD BEEN TO another world. Twice.

This wasn't another world like Venus or Mars. Nor was it the sort of 'other world' that adults might enthuse about as they walk around a big old house that has cherubs painted on the walls, outsize chandeliers and a signed photo of the Prime Minister on a piano. Edwin's 'other world' was exactly that – it wasn't even in our universe. The kingdom of Hysteria was in another track of time.

After careful consideration, Edwin didn't think that almost having his head chopped off or being forced to wear tights were the worst parts of his adventures. In Hysteria he'd become a prince and the worst thing about being royalty was going back to real life. If Edwin's family *knew* he'd been known as Prince Auvlin, heir to the throne of Hysteria, would they still treat him like a second class citizen?

'Last year's return to form continues, Edwin,' Mrs Spencer declared. She looked down her nose at his Autumn Term report, holding the sides between each forefinger and thumb.

'Bad reports are *not* radioactive, mum,' Edwin said with a sigh.

His oldest sister, Jenny, beamed. 'That one might as well be,' she snorted. 'Because it STINKS!'

Katie, his other sister, laughed so loud that she spat a piece of chewed-up chicken onto the table.

'Ugh . . .' Edwin moaned. 'I might not be the brain of Britain like you three,' – he shot a glance at Ollie, his younger brother – 'but at least I've got table manners!'

Mrs Spencer picked up the piece of poultry in a tissue and threw it into the bin. 'That's as may be, Edwin,' she said, 'but top grades are just as important.'

'Look,' Edwin said. 'You should know by now that I'm never going to be like *this* lot.'

'I don't see why not!' Mrs Spencer replied. Her nostrils flared and her bleached moustache quivered on her upper lip.

Edwin stood up. 'I'm just different. *They* got all the brains. One numpty out of four ain't bad. Right?'

'That's the first sensible thing you've said in ages!' Jenny squealed. 'I don't know why Perpetua Allbright bothers with you. She's so clever . . . what on Earth do you have to talk about?'

Edwin bit his lip. Perpetua had been to Hysteria too. She could be a first-class know-it-all, but he'd trust her with his life.

Edwin wearily left the room and trudged up the stairs. It was at times like this that he *longed* to go back to Hysteria. He knew his rightful place was here on Earth, with his family, but there he felt appreciated. Edwin lay on his bed and tucked his arms behind his head. It wasn't *only* because he'd helped the Hysterians by taking the place of Prince Auvlin. They'd needed Edwin because he looked exactly like their supposedly dead heir to the throne, but once he was there, the Hysterians discovered what kind of boy he was – brave, loyal and, in his own way, quite clever.

'Ollie, that is marvellous,' Mrs Spencer cooed from downstairs and Edwin kicked the door shut. He sat up. There was still the family tree homework to finish. He was enjoying learning all about his family from years ago and it would take his mind off the bunch of raving braniacs downstairs.

Edwin stood on the bed and took down two large boxes from the top of his wardrobe. His mother had given them to him for research and they contained all sorts – certificates, hundreds of photos, old insurance policies, some medals from the First World War. . . Edwin needed to find out the name of his grandfather's grandfather and quickly scanned through a succession of official-looking papers.

Nothing. He rifled through the rest of the box until he came to a large plastic bag at the bottom. Peering inside, he found four small bags. He took one out. Inside were some little labels – the sort tied around the wrists of newborn babies.

'Katherine Olga Wendy,' Edwin read. He huffed. 'KOW . . . wrong spelling if you ask me.'

The bag also contained some mittens and a small white teddy bear. Edwin moved onto the next one, which held the same stuff but for Oliver. And then for Jenny. Edwin held the last bag up. Should he bother looking at it? It would only be the same thing . . .

But Edwin frowned. This bag was heavier than the rest. He upended it and the contents spilled onto the bed. There was the name label: Edwin Ernest Luke. Good job he'd managed to keep that quiet. But something else caught his eye. A cone-shaped piece of metal – maybe a piece of jewellery . . . something that might hang on a chain. Edwin picked the piece up and put it in his left hand. It was *really* heavy – too heavy for silver. There was a peculiar woven pattern on it and tiny, almost indistinguishable etchings at one end . . .

Within a few seconds Edwin's palm began to heat up. Gasping, he threw the pendant down, but his hand grew warmer still. Edwin sprang to his feet. There was a sudden crackle and sparks began to fly in mid-air. They flashed bright white and the space between blurred like static on an old TV. There was a buzzing that grew louder then softer. Edwin could hear snippets of other sounds, as if a radio was being tuned in.

Then something came into view. The image was a little shaky, but the thing standing in front of Edwin was what he'd take to be . . . a *ghost*!

It was a tall, thin figure, wearing a dark hooded shroud that was tied at the waist with rope. The deep hood hung low and Edwin could only see the lower half of an almost skeletal face. The lips were unnaturally dark and they moved rapidly, as if they were chanting the same thing over and over again. Patches of words punctured the hissing, but Edwin couldn't make out what was being said.

'What d'you want?' Edwin managed to gabble. 'Who are you?'

The figure didn't pause for breath. It just carried on talking. Had it heard what Edwin had said? Did it even know he was there?

Edwin put his hand out, extending it slowly and shakily towards the image, only for his fingers to waft straight through it. Nothing but warm air. Edwin knelt down, trying to look under the hood, but all he could see was shadow. Something this weird could only mean one thing.

Edwin swallowed, then said, 'Are you from Hysteria?'

The body remained still with only the lips moving. The buzzing softened and for a few seconds the image seemed to stick and replay with the sound of a rhythmical 'tic . . . tic . . . tic'. Then it jolted back to life before the image began to fade. The sparks fizzled out and the hissing shrank away. Edwin took a deep breath and leaned back against the wardrobe, his chest pounding. He'd never seen a ghost before, not in either world.

'Crikey . . .' he whispered. That pendant thing *had* to be from Hysteria. So what was it doing in his parents' house? And how long had it been here?

Edwin placed a pillow over the pendant, pulled on his trainers and fumbled for his mobile phone. *Meet me in the park*, he texted. *URGENT* . He pressed SEND, and hoped that Perpetua wasn't too busy.

CHAPTER TWO

EDWIN WAS WAITING BY THE swings. He'd stood near the roundabout first, but two little kids had asked him to push it, then complained he wasn't quick enough. Edwin had told them to get lost and one of them had starting crying. Now he felt *awful*.

It was only a few minutes before he spotted Perpetua hurtling towards him like an express train.

'I take it this is not Earth related,' Perpetua said as she put on the brakes.

"Course not! I never get excited about anything round here.'

Perpetua took off her glasses. 'Before you tell me, have you remembered to do your chemistry homework?'

'Yep,' Edwin said impatiently. Perpetua might be super brainy, but she had a shallow grasp on the meaning of 'URGENT'. 'It's in my rucksack for tomorrow.'

'How long did it take?'

'I dunno. An hour maybe . . .'

'And did you understand it?'

'Nope.'

Perpetua sighed and folded her arms. 'Edwin,' she said. 'What *are* we going to do with you?'

'Don't *you* start,' Edwin replied.

'Sorry.' Perpetua said, without sounding as if she were sorry at all. 'Right – tell me what's happened.'

Edwin glanced around. 'Let's go on the swings. Once we get going, anyone who comes near will only be able to hear every other word.'

They sat side by side, Perpetua making sure she moved in time with Edwin. 'Get on with it,' she hissed. 'I can't stand the suspense!'

'Right,' Edwin began, making sure he didn't swing too high. 'But I warn you . . . this is weird.'

Perpetua frowned. 'Weirder than you taking the place of a dead prince who is lying in a mausoleum, but then comes back to life?' she gabbled. 'Weirder than going to another world that's almost medieval but whose time moves faster than ours? Weirder –'

'OK! I get the point.' Edwin said. 'Now . . . . I was looking through some old boxes today for the family tree homework –'

'Have you finished *that*?' Perpetua butted in.

Edwin sighed. Was she ever going to let him finish? Or *start*, even? 'Whaddaya think? I said I was *looking through some old boxes* . . .'

'*I've* already finished it.'

'Getaway,' Edwin said flatly. 'As I was saying – I was looking through some stuff, and I found a bag that had some bits and pieces from when I was born. There was one for each of us four kids.'

'So?'

'Well, Jenny's bag had some glove things and a little teddy. And Ollie's had a picture with me and dad, and Katie's was like that, too. But mine . . .' Edwin trailed off. He wasn't sure if what he was about to say was too incredible. 'Mine contains a small piece of jewellery – a pendant or something. From the look of it I reckon it might come from Hysteria.'

Perpetua looked at Edwin as if he had lost his mind. 'That's ridiculous!' she scoffed. 'How could something from there have got into your baby bag? We only went to Hysteria for the first time *two* years ago. We'd never even heard of the place before then!'

'I know that,' Edwin replied patiently. 'But the Hysterians can rewind our time, can't they? Maybe they rewound it fourteen years and someone came to my house and planted this thing and then . . .' He shrugged. 'And then . . . I don't know what would've happened.'

'I'll tell you what,' Perpetua said quickly. 'We'd have

lived through all of those fourteen years for a second time – the world would've had a mass deja vu on a grand scale!' She shook her head. 'After we've been to Hysteria they've rewound weeks for us so we wouldn't be missed. But *that* long – I don't think so.'

Edwin hadn't even told Perpetua the worst of it. 'I told you all this was weird. But there's something else . . .'

'What does this pendant look like? Are you sure it's Hysterian? Can I see?'

'I didn't bring it – I promised my mum I wouldn't take anything from the boxes out of the house. Anyway, when I –'

'Why did she say that?'

'That's the sort of thing mothers *do*, isn't it? They keep important stuff safe . . . My mum seems to have kept most stuff from when we were little, so she probably doesn't want anything to get lost.' Edwin crossed his arms. 'Now, listen to me – this is the *really* weird bit – when I picked up this pendant, a kind of ghost thing appeared right in front of me.'

Perpetua was dumbstruck and Edwin took full advantage. 'It was a figure with a hood. It looked a bit like a monk, but I couldn't see its eyes. And it was saying something really quickly, over and over. I wasn't sure if it even knew I was there . . . but what if it was trying to tell me something?'

Perpetua blinked. 'Do you believe in ghosts, Edwin?'

Edwin hesitated. 'I don't think I *did*,' he replied

carefully. 'But if someone had told me about Hysteria before I went there, I wouldn't have believed in that either.'

'But what if this thing you've found isn't Hysterian? What if it's *Umbrian*?'

Edwin swallowed. In the back of his mind *he'd* wondered if the pendant could also come from Umbria – the sworn enemy of Hysteria – but he hadn't allowed himself to say it out loud.

Perpetua suddenly shot to her feet. 'I have to see the pendant! I have to see it now! I have to see it *this second*!'

Edwin jumped off the swing. 'What is this – *Star Trek*? Sorry, but I've left the teleporting machine in my wardrobe.'

'You know what I mean. Come on. Hurry!' Perpetua hurtled across the grass to the park gates with Edwin trailing in her wake.

As Edwin approached his front door he shot a look at Perpetua. 'Right, we get in and go straight to my room to look at the pendant. OK? Don't let my mum start talking to you or we'll be there till Christmas.'

'Right,' Perpetua said, looking slightly jumpy. Even she was a little unnerved by the force of nature that was Mrs Spencer.

As Edwin closed the door he could hear the radio

blaring in the kitchen. Mrs Spencer was listening to the 'Bring out the Prodigy in Your Child' tape again. Edwin knew it well. They had five minutes to get to his room – plenty of time.

Edwin jerked his head and he and Perpetua crept up the stairs. Luck was on their side: Jenny and Katie were in their bedroom screaming at each other, and Ollie was playing solo badminton in the dining room.

As Edwin reached the landing, Jenny cried, 'THAT IS NOT YOUR T-SHIRT!'

'YES IT SO IS!' Katie squealed.

There was prolonged muffled struggling, then the unmistakable sound of a gigantic RIP!

'AAAAGHHHH! You did that on purpose!'

'No I didn't. And even if I *did*, it serves you right!'

Edwin grimaced and hustled Perpetua into his room.

'Goodness,' she said. 'Are your sisters always like that?'

'Nah,' Edwin said, plonking himself down on the bed. 'Sometimes they *really* get on each others' nerves.' He picked up a pair of socks from the floor and pulled one over each hand.

'Edwin, what are you doing?' Perpetua asked.

'I thought I'd play sock puppets,' Edwin replied. Then, 'Duh! Call yourself a genius? I'm not gonna take the chance of touching the pendant again, am I? If what you said was right – who's to say it isn't from Umbria?'

Edwin removed the pillow, relieved to find the

pendant still there underneath. He threw the pillow to one side then looked at Perpetua.

'Go on,' he urged. 'Have a look.'

Perpetua peered at the pendant and put her hand out, then corrected herself. 'D'you think I should touch it?'

Edwin pulled a face. 'Not unless you want the fright of your life.'

There was a little pause, and Edwin knew exactly what Perpetua was going to do. Too curious to be cautious, she brushed a fingertip against the pendant, waited, then went back for a few more seconds. Edwin steeled himself, but nothing happened – no ghostly figure appeared.

Perpetua withdrew her hand. 'It doesn't feel warm to me.'

'But you didn't hold it like I did.' He scratched his head. 'Not that I want you to . . . I don't wanna see that thing again.'

'Are you didn't just dream it?'

Edwin sighed. 'You don't think I can tell the difference between what's real and a dream? Gimme a break! I'm not as stupid as you think I am.'

'Sorry,' Perpetua chimed, putting her hands on her hips. 'Well, I couldn't feel anything. Although it certainly *looks* as if it might come from Hysteria or Umbria.' She stood up and peeked into one of Edwin's boxes, her eyes suddenly widening. 'Oh my goodness! What is *that*?'

'What? What?' Edwin said quickly, scrambling to his feet. Had he missed something? Was there some other Umbrian artefact lurking in his bedroom? He leaned over the box and looked inside.

'Oh,' Edwin said with relief. 'It's a photo from my parents' wedding.'

He had, of course, seen the picture before but not for some time, and Edwin could still appreciate how startled Perpetua must have felt.

Mrs Spencer had always been very tall and Mr Spencer very short, but never was the difference more evident than on their wedding day, when Mrs Spencer wore outrageously high heels. She had too much hair and he had none, although she had more than enough teeth for both of them. All the bridesmaids were Mrs Spencer's sisters and, to be fair, she was the looker of the bunch.

'I don't think I've ever seen anything quite like it,' Perpetua murmured.

'My gran always said it was a *brilliant* day. She used to boast that complete strangers took pictures outside the church,' said Edwin.

Perpetua blinked. 'I bet they did.' She took a hanky out of her pocket and used it to pick up the pendant. 'I think we need to ask your mother about this.'

Edwin *really* didn't want to, but he led the way downstairs. The self-help tape had finished and Edwin walked into the kitchen to find Mrs Spencer with his chemistry exercise book in her hand.

'Ah . . . I was just about to write you a note. Have you spent enough time on this?' she asked Edwin sharply. 'From what I can see your theories have some glaring errors.'

'Hello, Mrs Spencer!'

Perpetua breezed into the room and Mrs Spencer's face brightened.

'Perpetua! I didn't know you were here. How are you? How are your grades?'

'As brilliant as ever,' Perpetua said keenly. She held out her hand and opened the hanky to show Mrs Spencer what she was holding without encouraging her to touch it. 'Edwin has got a few things to ask you about this. Haven't you, Edwin?'

Mrs Spencer looked at the pendant, stepped forward and reached out. 'What is that?' she said slowly. Perpetua tried to back away, but Mrs Spencer was too quick.

Edwin scrunched his eyes. *Don't take it . . . don't take it*, he pleaded silently.

Too late! 'Did you find this in one of the boxes?' Mrs Spencer said, picking it up.

'Yes!' Edwin said, just managing to contain himself. His mother's hand would start warming up any second . . . 'It was, er . . . in a bag . . . with some baby things,' he gabbled.

'Of course,' Mrs Spencer said, examining the pendant closely. 'I remember this appeared the day after you were born.'

Edwin blinked hard. Couldn't she feel the heat yet?

'Lots of people came to see you, and after they'd gone your father found this in your cot,' Mrs Spencer continued. 'We assumed it was some sort of gift. Your father and I didn't like it – we thought it looked rather cheap, but even as a new baby it seemed to fascinate you. Back then, I was convinced you were even brighter than the girls. I wonder what went wrong?'

Edwin stood there, staring. Where was the ghostly figure? First Perpetua had touched the pendant, then his mother had held it. Why hadn't anything happened?

'Do you, er, d'you *still* think it looks a bit cheap?' Perpetua said casually. 'I mean, would you mind if we studied it? We've been looking at metals in science.'

Mrs Spencer gave a beaming smile. 'Why not,' she replied, dropping the pendant back into the hanky. She creased her nose. 'I don't think it's a *precious* metal. It's certainly not silver.'

'That's really kind of you, Mrs Spencer,' Perpetua said, and she bolted back up the stairs. Edwin rushed after her to find her sitting on his bed with the pendant in the palm of her hand, no hanky in sight.

'Our conversation with your mother confirmed two things,' she said firmly. 'One, this relic – or whatever it is – has been in your family ever since you were born. And two, the ghostly apparition associated with it appears only to you.'

Edwin wasn't quite sure how he felt about this. He

loved Hysteria and everyone in it – especially King Janus – but the Ancient Relics he'd encountered before had brought nothing but trouble. This one, with its resident ghost, already seemed more trouble than most.

'What you said earlier,' Edwin said thoughtfully. 'That the pendant could be from Umbria. If it was, and has been in my house for all this time, wouldn't it have caused some problems somewhere down the line?' Edwin didn't need to explain what he meant: Perpetua knew very well that everything the Umbrians stood for was evil.

'You'd think so,' Perpetua replied. 'Or would we be jumping to conclusions?' She looked at the pendant then sighed in what seemed like an exaggerated way. 'I wonder how we can find out more about it?'

Perpetua was always looking for reasons to go back to Hysteria. Edwin chose to prolong her agony a little longer.

'Yeah,' he said, rubbing his chin. 'I can't think what we need to do. There's no way we can find anything out about it here. We can't ask anyone's advice. Hmmm . . .' Edwin scratched his head. 'What *can* we do?'

Perpetua stared at Edwin, looking if she were about to burst. Her eyes grew wider by the second, her lips pushed together like a towel wringing through a mangle. The last time Edwin had seen her like this, Mr Harper had told her to stop answering questions in class and give someone else a chance. Afterwards, Perpetua had said it had been the longest Physics lesson of her life.

Edwin smirked. 'D'you want to go back to Hysteria?'

'GOOD IDEA!' Perpetua blurted.

'Like you hadn't thought of it already. Thing is,' he said, 'how do we get to Hysteria without them asking us first? Both times, *they* came to *me*.'

For once, Perpetua looked stumped. 'We have no way of contacting them – unless there's something you haven't told me.'

'What d'you mean?'

'I know how close you and King Janus became. I just thought that maybe you had some way of getting in touch with him?'

Edwin had almost thought of Janus as his father, especially the last time he'd been to Hysteria.

'Nah,' Edwin replied, looking down. 'I've got no way of contacting Janus.'

'I need to put my thinking cap on,' Perpetua said.

'I thought you never took it off.'

Perpetua smiled broadly. 'That's very good, Edwin! I'll have to remember that one.'

They both spent quite a while thinking. Edwin started off thinking about the pendant, then found his thoughts straying to the goals he'd seen his team score last weekend. He stirred and asked himself how old the pendant could be, then wondered how many jelly beans he could fit into his 'I'm a Champion Nose-Picker' mug.

Perpetua suddenly clapped her hands. 'Are you thinking what I'm thinking?' she said.

'I doubt it.'

'Hmmm,' Perpetua agreed. 'I was thinking about the Amanthan Amulet. *That* came from Umbria and whenever you wore it the Umbrians knew how far away from them you were . . .'

There was a knock at the front door. Edwin hoped it was one of his mother's friends who would help keep her occupied.

'So now, you *definitely* think this pendant thing is Umbrian? That there's *Shadow* Magic in it?' Edwin said.

'Not necessarily!' Perpetua said. 'The Hysterians had a Protector of the Relics, right? Saleena. She knew if anything unusual was happening to them and if anyone was *touching* them.'

It slowly dawned on Edwin what Perpetua was on about. 'So relics send out a kind of signal . . .' Edwin trailed off. 'But Saleena died.'

Perpetua shook her head. 'And you think she hasn't been replaced? She performed a vital role – they're *bound* to have a new Protector of the Relics. If we touch the pendant, this person might be able to sense it and know that it's right here, in Templeton Grove. They'll put two and two together, then send for us!'

'Ed-WIN!' Mrs Spencer suddenly shouted from downstairs.

Edwin didn't respond. 'What d'you mean, 'if' we touch it?' he hissed. '*Three* of us already have!'

'Exactly,' Perpetua whispered. 'So they may already know what we've done. *And* they'll be getting the vortex ready to come and get us, and—' She suddenly stopped and grabbed Edwin's arm. 'Do you need to go to the bathroom?'

Edwin was outraged. 'What? D'you think I'm three years old or something!'

'I don't mean *that*,' she snapped. 'Twice before the vortex has appeared in your bathroom.'

There was a sudden rap on Edwin's door and it flew open. 'There's someone here to see you, Edwin,' Mrs Spencer said sharply. 'I've never laid eyes on him before but he says he's a school friend. He doesn't seem to be able to tell me his name.'

'Whaaaat?' Edwin moaned. This was all he needed. His mother left the room and he looked at Perpetua. 'I hope it's not that weird kid from Year Seven who moved in across the road. He keeps coming round.'

'Only one way to find out.'

They both shuffled onto the landing. There was a fairly tubby boy standing in the hall. His jeans were far too long and he was wearing a purple baseball cap. Edwin glanced at Perpetua and shrugged, 'Hello?'

The boy looked up and smiled.

'Hello,' he said softly.

It was a few seconds before Edwin and Perpetua took

in exactly who it was. Then at the same moment they scrambled downwards and grabbed their Hysterian friend and swept him up the stairs.

'Well . . . who is it?' Mrs Spencer called from the kitchen.

'It's Barry from Year Seven,' Edwin screeched. 'He's big for his age.'

They bundled into Edwin's room. Perpetua slammed the door and started to giggle.

'*Bellwin*, what *do* you look like?'

Bellwin glanced down at himself; he was a young wizard of Hysteria, and had never been to Earth before. 'I *hoped* I looked like I was from your kingdom. Did I get it right?'

'Sort of,' Edwin coughed. 'Baseball caps are a bit last century.'

Perpetua grabbed Bellwin and squeezed him into an enormous hug. 'It's so nice to see you! Have you come to take us back?'

'You have been expecting me?'

Perpetua opened her hand, and Bellwin's eyes widened.

'The relic *is* here,' Bellwin said with relief. 'Janus was told it was in another world, and this was the only place we could think of . . .'

'What sort of relic is it?' Perpetua asked keenly.

'We do not know,' Bellwin replied. 'The Protector sensed it was being handled, but was unable to tell what it was. Janus hopes to find out more when he looks at it.'

Edwin scratched his head. 'He might be in for a surprise.'

When a puzzled Bellwin looked for more answers, Perpetua looked at Edwin and shook her head. He changed the subject. 'Shall we get going? Bellwin, where's the vortex?'

'I need to summon it.'

Edwin and Perpetua exchanged a look then backed away slightly. They'd seen Bellwin get Hysterian spells wrong before. But he straightened his back and took a deep breath. 'Vortex alluminum!'

There was a sudden, very loud bang. The house rocked. This time Bellwin had got it right. Edwin was shunted to one side and Perpetua was dumped on the bed.

'Oh, crikey!' she screamed. 'Your mum will wonder what's happening . . .'

But Perpetua had forgotten that no one else could see or hear the vortex – only they three were tuned into its track of time. The rumbling gradually receded and an orange glow began to flicker in the corner of the room, growing wider and wider like flames licking at the centre of a newspaper.

Perpetua looked around the room. 'Before we go, have you got a bag?' she said in a hurry. 'We need to put the pendant somewhere safe . . .'

Edwin grabbed a rucksack and Perpetua popped the

relic in an inside pocket. Edwin did up every zip he could find and threw the straps over his shoulders. The vortex was now its full size, spitting huge sparks and filling the room with smoke.

'This one seems a bit angry,' Edwin coughed. 'Have you brought it through all right, Bellwin?'

'I think so, my friend,' Bellwin said, although he looked slightly nervous.

'Hello!' a voice boomed from the vortex.

Edwin and Perpetua instinctively huddled together.

'We are here, Master!' Bellwin cried.

'Ollwin!' Edwin squeaked.

'Edwin, How marvellous to hear you. I have no doubt that Perpetua is by your side?'

'Of course,' Perpetua said. She looked at Edwin and grinned, then they both realised they were holding hands. The pair coughed and stepped apart.

'You both sound splendid! But we have something of a mystery here . . . and I do believe you may be able to help us.'

'You mean the pendant?' Edwin said.

There was a pause.

'It seems you have been expecting us,' Ollwin said, sounding a little disgruntled not to be the one to reveal the mystery. 'The vortex is ready . . . we await you,' he added grandly.

Edwin closed his eyes and took in the deepest of breaths. There was no feeling like going back to Hysteria.

He looked at Perpetua and beamed. She grabbed his hand and this time he didn't struggle.

'Jump in!' Edwin whispered and they walked towards the shining circle.

CHAPTER THREE

CONSIDERING THIS WAS EDWIN AND Perpetua's fifth journey through the vortex, they didn't handle it well. They stepped gingerly into the haze and stood for a few seconds as if wearing new roller skates, waiting for the first slip.

Bellwin followed, but as he stepped in he tripped on his jeans. The pull along the tunnel of fire came just as he landed, throwing everything into disarray. Edwin's legs were taken from under him and he started the journey feet first. He grabbed Perpetua's arm and she streamed after him, closely followed by Bellwin who was facing the other way.

The heat seemed to take Perpetua by surprise and she

clamped her mouth shut, looking at Edwin as if it were his fault she was unprepared.

Edwin was busy trying to fly in a straight line. The power of the vortex pulled them through, of course, but if they didn't keep in their knees and elbows it could get messy. There was far more turbulence than usual, and Edwin imagined that he, Perpetua and Bellwin must look like pinballs ricocheting from here to there with an 'Oomph!' and an 'Oooouch!'

'I do not like this,' Bellwin gasped. 'It was very different on the first journey . . .'

'Where's the cold bit!' Perpetua demanded breathlessly, and just at that moment the air turned chilly, and fiery blasts were replaced with a high-pitched whistle. Both Edwin and Perpetua remembered to lie back, but Bellwin kept flailing around. Although they were travelling at quite a speed, it felt like Edwin was floating. He began to nod off, but then heard Perpetua murmur, 'Yes Daddy, the Five Year plan . . . early GCSEs . . . Baccalaureate . . . off to Cambridge.' She sighed. 'Or should I follow in your footsteps to Oxford?'

Bellwin, however, wasn't having such a good time. 'No . . . no!' he wailed. 'It was not supposed to turn into a rabbit's ear . . . it should have been a wooden spoon! How is Cook going to stir the soup now?'

Edwin smiled then let himself drift away. He could see the school day out at Bailton Adventure Towers. 'Whoa!' he whispered, raising his arms with the loop of a rollercoaster. 'Yippee! My lunch is staying put . . . I'm not gonna be sick!'

Nothing ever seemed to prepare Edwin for landing in Hysteria. They hit the ground with a thump – quite enough to wake them all up straightaway, but they still took a few seconds to come around. Edwin thought they'd land in the same field as before and he had to shake his head when his surroundings weren't as light as he expected.

'Must be cloudy,' he said, rubbing his eyes.

'No, Edwin,' Perpetua said, scrabbling to her feet. 'It's a darker place. A much, *much*, darker place.'

She grabbed Edwin's hand and pulled him up. They were standing at the mouth of a cave. Densely packed trees were all around, leaving only partial natural light to fall on the spot where they stood. The cave itself looked quite deep, and once Edwin's eyes had adjusted, he was able to see a little way in.

'Bellwin,' Perpetua said. 'Do you know *why* we haven't gone to the field again?'

Bellwin threaded his fingers. 'There may be two causes,' he replied. 'First, I was not standing properly when I entered the vortex, and it may have misaligned things.' He coughed. 'Second, I believe that the vortex took you from another room in your house before – what you call the bathroom? Well, this time we went from your bedroom, and the small distance between the two may have caused us to go off course.'

Edwin narrowed his eyes. 'The first vortex we ever travelled in showed up in a storage cupboard school,' he said slowly. 'We landed in the right field *that* time.'

'Oh, well in that case,' Bellwin said matter-of-factly, 'it is purely my fault.'

Perpetua bent down and picked two small white flowers from a clump of grass. 'These,' she said, holding them up, 'only grow in the Inigo Forest – you told me that, didn't you Bellwin? So at least we're in Hysteria. Look, there's a lot more of them in that cave. Maybe it's the soil, or the lack of light . . .'

Edwin gave a broad grin as Perpetua wandered off for a closer look. It was at times like these he was glad that Perpetua had a memory like a laptop. But she didn't have his brilliant sense of direction. 'That means we're not that far from the field. I just need to work out which bit of the forest we're in.' He took a few strides into the trees. 'Let's get a move on. We'll try this way f—'

'EDWIN!'

Edwin spun on his heel and dashed back to find Perpetua fleeing the mouth of the cave.

'What is the matter?' Bellwin said.

'Bones . . . bones . . . in the cave,' Perpetua spluttered.

'Human bones?' Bellwin gasped.

When Perpetua nodded Edwin's mouth dropped. 'You mean with a skull and a, er . . . jaw bone and . . . erm . . .'

'You mean the cranium and the mandible!' Perpetua

replied, almost hysterical. 'Yes! Yes! Yes! And femurs and clavicles and metatarsals and—'

Edwin gripped Perpetua's shoulders. 'This is no time for a biology lesson,' he said calmly. 'You found a whole human skeleton?'

'Not one!' Perpetua cried. She took a deep breath. 'There must be bones from half a dozen bodies in there!'

Edwin felt fear lurch into his stomach. Bodies meant trouble. And around here, trouble usually meant the Umbrians. Edwin swallowed and looked into Perpetua's eyes. Maybe if he stared at her long enough she might take that back. Maybe she might suddenly smile and say it was all a big joke . . . that there wasn't *really* anything to be worried about. But Edwin kept on staring, and Perpetua kept on looking as if she had just seen Jack the Ripper.

'Great!' Edwin finally let Perpetua go. 'It's been all of ten seconds since we stepped out of the vortex and already there's a blimmin' problem. We can't just turn up, give Janus this relic back, stay for a few days, have a nice time and see Janus and let everyone make a fuss of us and . . .' Edwin stopped babbling, and raised a hopeful finger in the air. 'But am I overreacting? Is this *really* a problem? Shall I have a look?'

Perpetua sniffed. 'I don't see why not, although I don't see how likely it is that finding human remains in a cave can be anything other than bad news. But you're not going back in there without me. Bellwin – are you going to come too?'

'Er . . . yes, of course.'

'The more the merrier,' Edwin said. 'Call me old fashioned, but the thought of being alone with a load of skeletons ain't that appealing.'

Perpetua let Edwin go in first, but was close on his heels. 'They're just a few metres in, on the right,' she whispered.

The further Edwin crept into the cave, the slower his feet moved. The darker it got, the less he wanted to see what Perpetua had discovered. Edwin suddenly stopped. There were hundreds of bones visible over one side of the cave, scattered around a large patch of dirt. It was easy to spot the seven skulls.

'I though you said it was six sets,' he said nervously. 'It looks to me as if there's one more than that.'

Perpetua crept alongside followed closely by Bellwin. 'I can count, Edwin, thank you very much! When *I* saw them, it was a bit of a surprise . . . I didn't hang around to do a stock take.'

Edwin tut-tutted. Sometimes Perpetua could be really tetchy. He looked back at the bones. There didn't seem to be any further into the cave where it started to get *really* dark. He crept a little further forward. There was no sign of clothing, or weapons.

'I wonder if these people were Hysterian?' Edwin said, feeling quite queasy.

'It's not like there's much here to go on,' Perpetua replied.

Edwin nodded. 'How long d'you reckon they've been dead?'

Perpetua took her glasses from her pocket and kneeled down. 'Well, it normally takes six months to a year for a body to decompose to the bone in the fresh air. After fifty years they would turn to dust.' She squinted and leant in closer. 'Let's take one of these outside for better look.'

Edwin pulled a face. 'You're gonna pick one up?'

'Yes, of course I am. All these people are dead. There's nothing else in here – no monsters lurking anywhere.' She pushed her glasses up her nose. 'If one of these bodies were remotely fresh then I *would* be worried. Have you got a hanky or something?'

Edwin baulked. Did he look like the sort of boy that carried around a tissue on purpose? He took off his rucksack, rooted around inside and pulled out a copy of *GOAL!* Magazine. He tore off the back cover.

'Use *this*,' he said manfully.

Perpetua picked up a bone and turned to the mouth of the cave. Edwin and Bellwin followed. The light outside still wasn't brilliant, but it seemed enough for Perpetua.

'There's hardly any degeneration of the bone,' she said, almost to herself. 'They can't have been here for years and years. Maybe only a few . . .'

Edwin cleared his throat and tried to think of something useful to say. He couldn't think of anything.

'We can all have a good look at that later.' Perpetua wrapped the bone in the magazine cover and popped it into Edwin's rucksack. 'Right – what are we going to tell Ollwin?'

'I don't think we should say anything about anything until we see Janus. We don't wanna have to repeat the same stories a million times,' Edwin said, figuring one more secret wouldn't hurt for now.

'I think that is very wise,' Bellwin said. 'Let us go.'

'OK. Let's get going then . . . Ollwin will be wondering where we are.'

The last time Edwin was in Hysteria he'd taken part in an orienteering competition, so he knew this forest very well. It didn't take him long to get his bearings and within half an hour he'd found the clearing they needed.

'Oh, look!' Perpetua squealed, emerging from the trees. 'There's Ollwin . . . he's got horses!'

Edwin broke into a broad grin and quickened his pace. As he approached the Hysterian High Wizard, Edwin saw that old man looked much the same: grey-haired, short, rotund and with the kind expression that belonged to everyone's favourite grandfather.

'We're here at last!' Perpetua called. She ran up to

Ollwin and planted a kiss on his cheek. 'I'm sorry we've kept you waiting.'

'Dear Perpetua,' Ollwin said, blushing. 'My patience has been rewarded with the sight of you!' He strode to Edwin and clapped him firmly on the back. 'Your third time in Hysteria, my friend. This is becoming a regular occurrence.'

'It is a happy day when our friends from Earth arrive in Hysteria,' Bellwin beamed.

'Sorry we didn't land here, Ollwin,' Edwin said. 'But the vortex didn't come to exactly the same place as before.'

'Well, you are here now. That is all that matters. So, tell me . . . how are you both?'

Edwin opened his mouth to answer, but Perpetua blurted. 'Oh, we're fine, Ollwin. Things are much the same at school. I'm doing terribly well . . . Edwin is performing below national average expectations.'

'Why don't you big me up a bit more!' Edwin said crossly.

Perpetua bit her lip. 'Oh, sorry.' She turned to Ollwin. 'He means why don't I talk about him in very positive terms *again*. He doesn't really mean that, of course, because I didn't talk about him positively in the first place. He's being sarcastic, you see.' She gave a weak smile. 'Which means . . .'

Edwin crossed his arms.

'Perhaps I'll explain that later,' Perpetua said quietly.

'Anyway,' Edwin said. 'It's great to be back!'

Ollwin rubbed his hands together. 'And this time for nothing more than to fetch something to us. You have the relic, my boy?'

'Yeah,' Edwin replied. 'It's safe here in my bag.'

'Good! There is a little mystery involved, but with your help we hope to solve it. There is certainly no danger apparent.'

Perpetua and Bellwin looked at Edwin, who pulled a bemused face.

They mounted their horses and Edwin steered towards Bellwin. 'So, how's the magic going?' Edwin asked. 'It's two years since you got Full Wizarding, you must be flying by now . . .'

Bellwin glanced cautiously at Ollwin. 'Er . . . yes. I am always kept busy. I start training an apprentice of my own tomorrow.'

'I will add that it is not my idea,' Ollwin said. 'Once again King Janus chose to reward Bellwin for his part in our defence of Hysteria against the Umbrians.'

'But mine was such a *small* part of our victory,' Bellwin added. '*I* would never have guessed the Umbrian army was made up of clones *or* known how to defeat them. I am not as much help to Hysteria as you, Edwin.'

Ollwin kicked his horse into a trot. 'We can discuss this on the way back to the castle, Bellwin. His Majesty asked us to hurry back – he is looking forward to seeing both our young friends.'

CHAPTER FOUR

As SOON AS THE TOPMOST turrets of Emporium Castle appeared over the horizon, Edwin's heart began to race. Perpetua and Bellwin were chatting to him, but all he really wanted to do was gaze at the grey stone towers as they grew closer and closer. There was the east wing . . . the west wing . . . and the gallery, the highest room in the castle. This was Edwin's favourite place in the world – in *any* world.

As they approached the entrance the tall wooden doors started to grind backwards and Edwin nudged Perpetua's leg with his shoe and leaned over.

'Not mentioning the ghost or the bones until we see Janus, right?' he said quietly.

'That's fine,' Perpetua said, flicking her hair over her shoulder. 'Janus should be one of the first to hear about it. He is the king, after all.'

Ollwin kicked his horse into a trot and the rest clip-clopped behind over the cobbles and through to an inner courtyard. Edwin was hoping that Janus may be waiting for them there, but he wasn't, although what Edwin saw still brought a smile to his face.

Eifus and Driefus Gonk were standing there in a very grand pose, as if they were fashion models. Eifus towered above everyone and was wearing a tunic that was way too short; Driefus was incredibly tiny and was wearing one that was way too long.

'Edwin! Perpetua!' Eifus cried as they pulled their horses to a stop. 'In honour of your return to Hysteria, my brother and I have exchanged clothes for the day!' He yanked down the hem of his tunic.

Dreifus gathered up the folds of his tunic from the ground. 'Even though we are wearing each other's clothes they remain, of course, a perfect fit.' He beamed up at his brother. 'You will remember that we are twins.'

Eifus smiled down. 'Identical.'

'Good grief,' Perpetua giggled under her breath. 'How have they *still* not realised they look completely different?'

Edwin raised his eyebrows. 'They're about as old as my granddad,' he replied. 'If they haven't realised by now, they never will.'

Perpetua dismounted and gave her horse's reins to Bellwin. 'Every time I see you,' she said to the brothers, 'I think . . . that's . . . just . . . *amazing!*'

Eifus executed an extravagant bow and straightened up with a layer of dust covering his fluffy white hair. 'You are not alone. As you know, our likeness has been commented upon countless times, dear lady,' he said with a toothy grin.

Dreifus wiped his shiny bald head with a hanky. 'Oh, yes. When our dear departed mother was alive she could barely tell us apart.'

'Did you need to wear badges?' Edwin said with a grin.

'Yes, we did,' Eifus replied brightly. 'How *did* you guess?'

Ollwin coughed. 'Edwin has brought us the relic,' he said.

'Excellent!' Eifus and Dreifus exclaimed together.

'You know, Edwin,' said Eifus, stroking his beard. 'His Majesty saw fit to put *me* in charge of finding the relic.'

Dreifus put his hands on his hips. 'You, dear brother? I think you will find that ultimately *I* led the investigation.'

'His Majesty is a kindly monarch, and I'm sure he wanted to give you that *impression*,' Eifus said pompously. He put his hand into his cloak and produced a small box. 'This,' he added, turning to Edwin, 'is where we will place the relic to present it to Janus.' He blew on the box and a cloud of dust spun into the air.

'It is a Gonk family heirloom,' Dreifus spluttered, fending off a sneeze. 'Over the years it has been used to store many important and historical items.'

'Yes,' Eifus said wistfully. 'For example, our dear departed mother's betrothal ring. A splendid example of Meticullan metal work, which –'

'Which you lost,' Dreifus said pointedly.

Eifus didn't flinch. 'The original broach of the Gonk coat of arms. Several fine crystals were set into the design, which –'

Dreifus crossed his arms. 'Which you lost.'

Again Eifus ignored his twin. 'The deed to the family—'

'Which you—'

'Brother, dear!' Eifus snarled, turning on his heel. 'All those things are *not* lost. It is just that I have yet to find them!'

'Eifus and Dreifus!' Ollwin hissed. 'The King is waiting!'

Dreifus snatched the box from Eifus. 'Please place the relic in here, Edwin. It is a fitting receptacle for presentation to the king.' Dreifus put his nose in the air and opened the box with a theatrical flourish. He tipped it towards Edwin, and hundreds of toenail clippings tumbled to the ground.

'Oh! There they are!' Eifus cried. 'I have been looking for those everywhere!'

'Eifus!' Dreifus yelled. 'How long have those ghastly specimens been in our precious *family heirloom* box?'

Eifus shrugged. 'I have been searching for them for over five years . . .'

Dreifus sniffed. 'Did they get there by accident, or were you planning to bequeath them in your will?'

Eifus didn't answer, but scrabbled on the floor to collect up the clippings.

Perpetua looked at Edwin. 'Good source of DNA,' she said. 'But I think I'll be satisfied if my parents leave me the house.'

Dreifus tipped up the box and what remained of the crusty toenails landed in Eifus's hair. 'You can retrieve those later, brother dear.' He thrust the box at Edwin. 'Place the item in here, if you please.'

Edwin opened his rucksack and Perpetua rummaged inside then pulled out the relic. Edwin held his breath, but once again the ghostly hooded figure did not appear. Ollwin, Bellwin, Eifus and Dreifus all leaned in to take a closer look.

'It is smaller than I thought,' Ollwin said. 'Janus will be so pleased to have it returned to Hysteria.'

'Yes, I will give it to the king,' said Eifus.

'No, I will,' said Dreifus.

'I said, I—'

'Enough!'

Everyone jumped at Ollwin's outburst.

'In the last few minutes I have had enough of your

bickering to last me a lifetime, *dear brothers.*' He turned to a side door. 'Now. Follow me!'

The walk to the Throne Room was one that Edwin loved. The slight chill from the stone walls, the flickering light from the flaming lanterns, the occasional echo from rooms far above . . . it all made Edwin's stomach flutter. This was Emporium Castle – there was nowhere else like it. It almost felt like coming home.

His excitement increased as the entrance to the Throne Room came into sight. Two guards stood either side, long spears clenched between their fists. Ollwin swept through and Edwin followed, eager to see who was there. The reds, greens and golds of the Throne Room banners dazzled as they passed into the bright light; and there, behind the golden throne, shone the soft muted light of the dormant vortex.

The figure occupying the throne stood up. Tall and broad, the king made an impressive figure as he quickly descended the steps to the stone floor. He walked quickly towards Edwin, his arms outstretched, his expression one of pure joy.

Edwin found himself running, his gaze fixed on the king's. His heart began to thump and he almost jumped into Janus's arms before warmth enveloped him.

'Hello,' Edwin croaked. He nudged his face into the king's long red hair and gave a contented sigh.

'Hello, my boy.' Janus hugged Edwin tight, then held him by the shoulders and stared. 'You have grown,' he said softly. 'It is wonderful to have you here in Emporium Castle.'

Edwin blinked furiously. 'It's good to be here, father . . . er, Your Majesty.'

The king smiled, and so did Edwin. There was nothing he had enjoyed more than playing this man's son.

'Good afternoon, Your Majesty!'

Perpetua sidled up to Edwin. 'It is OK if I come along, isn't it? I wasn't too much of a nuisance last time, and now Edwin actually doesn't seem to mind . . .'

The king released Edwin from his grasp and smiled broadly. 'You are always welcome, dear Perpetua.' He took her hand and kissed it. 'What would Hysteria be with Edwin, but without you?'

Perpetua blushed. 'Have *I* grown?' she said, almost standing on her tiptoes.

'Hmmm, I am not sure,' the king teased, winking at Edwin. 'But perhaps your brain is a little bigger than it was.'

Perpetua looked at Edwin and grinned. 'How lovely it is to be back!'

The king beckoned everyone to follow him to the other end of the hall, where Mersium stood by the side of the throne, even taller and broader than Janus, looking every inch the King's closest advisor and friend.

Primus, Janus's First Knight, was sitting on the steps that led up to the throne. His usual serious expression had given way to a smile.

But the other attendee didn't look very happy at all. Lorius, also Janus's advisor – who had brought Edwin and Perpetua to Hysteria the first time – looked as miserable and disapproving as ever.

Edwin glanced at Perpetua. 'Lorius is pleased to see us,' he whispered.

'So I see,' she replied. 'I do wish he'd cheer up a bit. If he wasn't so grumpy he might let me see some Hysterian science.'

Edwin pulled a face. 'Don't hold your breath. There's more chance of Henry VIII making you a sausage sandwich.'

Mersium and Primus descended the steps.

'You return to Hysteria again,' Primus said, shaking Edwin's hand. 'And we are all very glad to receive you.'

'How are you, Edwin?' Mersium asked. 'You too, Perpetua?'

'Oh, very excited to be back,' Perpetua gushed.

Lorius stepped forward. He looked from Edwin to Perpetua. 'Where is the relic?'

'Hello, Lorius,' said Edwin flatly. 'I'm fine thanks, how are you?' He jerked his head at Eifus and Dreifus. 'They've got it.'

The twins were standing closely together with their backs to everyone. Their bodies jerked quickly to one side, then back again. There was a muffled 'Aagghh,' then suddenly Dreifus fell and hit the floor.

'*I* will do it!' Eifus hissed, then spun around holding aloft the box with a toothy grin.

'Sire,' he said dramatically, 'I have fulfilled your wish and proudly present you with the missing relic.'

Dreifus picked himself up. '*You* did not bring it here,' he said, straightening the neck of his tunic. 'It was Edwin and Perpetua.' He rushed forward and clasped his brother's hand. 'We will both present the relic to the king,' he said, and bundled them both up to the throne.

Janus frowned and reached out for the box. He gripped one side, but the twins were too busy fighting to release it.

'Let it go! Let it go!' the king boomed. Eifus and Dreifus quickly took their hands away. They both overbalanced and fell to the floor side by side.

'Just another day in the life of the Gonks,' Edwin said, shaking his head. 'They should be on the telly . . . they'd make a fortune.'

'Leave us, Eifus and Dreifus,' Janus said, losing patience. 'Find something else to do.'

The brothers looked at each other. 'Could you pick the remains of the toenails from my hair, brother dear?' Eifus asked.

'Of course. With pleasure,' Dreifus replied. They stood up and bowed to the king.

'We are glad to be of service,' they chimed together,

then turned to scuttle from the hall.

'Yes, yes.' Janus waved his hand. 'And, er . . . thank you.' He looked at the box, then opened it. His face lit up in recognition. Edwin could see that some memories had been stirred.

'How could I forget?' the king said quietly. He took the relic from the box and held it up to the light. 'This belonged to Queen Ahven . . . it was a keepsake from her youth. I am glad it is returned to us.' Then he frowned. 'But my first questions are to you, Edwin: why was it in your house on Earth? And how did it get there?'

Suddenly Edwin felt under the spotlight. Everyone was looking at him, but he didn't have an answer. 'I really don't know,' he muttered. 'My mum said she found it on the bed in the hospital the day after I was born. After that, it was in a box in the loft for years.'

Everyone looked a bit puzzled. Perpetua coughed. 'A loft is the space in a house above the top floor but under the roof. It's like another sort of room really. Some people have a loft conversion to make it into a proper room – *my* parents did it.'

Edwin looked at her. 'We just keep junk in ours.'

Perpetua pushed her glasses up her nose. 'Junk,' she repeated. 'That's items that aren't really rubbish, but that no one wants to use any more.'

Bellwin put his hand up. 'And you still keep this *junk*?'

'Oh yes,' Perpetua replied matter-of-factly. 'But no one knows why.'

The Hysterians looked no less puzzled than they did before, and Ollwin was the next one to speak, seeming keen to put the conversation back on track. 'Edwin, your mother is sure the relic has been with you all those years?'

'That's what she said.'

Primus stepped forward. 'Your Majesty, when Prince Auvlin was born and Queen Ahven died, did the Keeper of the Relics say that the item had been disturbed? Are you able to remember?'

Janus shook his head. 'No, Primus. During the weeks and months after my wife's death my mind was submerged in grief. Saleena may have told me, of course, but if she did then I did not act upon it.'

Edwin glanced at Lorius. When they were there the last time, the only other person who had the password to gain access to see the Protector of the Relics was *him*.

'What about you, Lorius?' Edwin said, sounding a little blunt. 'Did Saleena tell *you*?'

Lorius looked at Edwin with his cold stare. 'Until the queen's death only she and Janus were able to see and instruct Saleena. After that, the king decided another person should take over from Queen Ahven. He chose me.'

'So when the relic disappeared, the only person Saleena could have told was the king,' Perpetua said.

She shrugged. 'Well, it being in Edwin's house doesn't seem to have caused a problem, does it?'

There were a few seconds of thought, then Primus said. 'It still worries me, Perpetua. A relic belonging to Hysterian royalty is found in another world . . . it could mean anything. Just because there is no apparent sign of danger, it does not mean there is none.'

Edwin winced. He and Perpetua had a couple of things to tell them that could put a whole different spin on this.

'Actually,' he said carefully. 'There's, er . . . there's some stuff you should probably know.'

'Something about the relic?' Janus asked.

'*One* of them yes . . . the other one, no.'

'Carry on,' Lorius said icily. Edwin glanced at Perpetua and rolled his eyes. He knew Lorius would think it'd all be *their* fault.

'Well,' Edwin began. 'When I found the relic, I picked it up, and . . . er . . . something appeared.'

'What was it?' Ollwin said quickly.

Edwin looked around the room and almost winced before he said, 'I think it was a ghost.' When there was silence he added, 'Does that sound really stupid?'

Janus shook his head. 'No, Edwin,' he said gravely. 'There are many in the territories who believe in the spirit world. My wife was one of them.'

Perpetua nodded. 'Well the spirit of Hereticus existed!' she said. 'And for all we know it probably still does.'

Lorius looked at her disdainfully. 'The use of Shadow Magic to extract spirits and the appearance of so-called ghosts are two different things.'

'Yes,' Perpetua agreed. 'But Hereticus did have to *die* before the Umbrian wizards could transfer his spirit into a live body. Only once he was a *ghost* could they use Shadow Magic.'

Lorius looked as if he were about to reply, but Janus cut in.

'The boy saw what the boy saw,' he said calmly. 'What is was is a matter of debate. What did this thing look like, Edwin?'

'A man . . . he was really skinny. He had a sort of robe on with a hood. There was some rope tied around the middle.' Edwin noticed the king's mouth open slightly. He looked almost confused. But Edwin carried on. 'The hood was over his face, so I couldn't see all of it. But it looked like he was saying the same thing over and over again.'

'Was he talking to *you*?' Janus asked.

Edwin shrugged. 'I dunno. I'm not sure he actually realised I was there.' He hesitated. 'D'you know who it is, Your Majesty?'

Janus briefly put his hand to his head, then nodded. 'That, Edwin, is how Ahven described her spirit guide.'

It was the last reply Edwin had been expecting. All he could whisper was, '*What*?'

But the king was looking at the relic again. 'I am

holding this, and the spirit guide has not appeared. Has anyone else held it?'

'Yes, Your Majesty,' Perpetua butted in. 'I have and Edwin's mother has. Nothing appeared to us, either.'

Janus locked his stare into Edwin's. 'So why is Ahven's spirit guide appearing to you?' he said slowly.

Edwin swallowed. 'I dunno.'

'How strange,' Ollwin said, wringing his hands and leaning closer. 'Can you hold the relic again, Edwin. Can we see what you saw?'

Janus held up his hand. 'Not yet,' he interrupted. 'There was something else you needed to tell us?'

Edwin, still reeling from what Janus had said, cleared his throat. 'Well, when Perpetua, Bellwin and I came through the vortex it didn't dump us in the usual place. We landed somewhere else and we found something.'

Primus's hand went to the helm of his sword. 'This sounds familiar . . .' he said slowly. 'Have you found *another* body?'

Bellwin coughed. 'Not one,' he said. 'But *seven*.'

Janus stood up. 'Seven bodies?' he gasped. 'Where were they . . . *who* were they?'

'When we say bodies,' Edwin replied, 'we mean more like bones. We found them in a cave in the Inigo Forest.'

'Skeletons? Ollwin said. 'So they had been dead for some time.'

Perpetua threaded her fingers. 'I had a close look,

and I think it's been a matter of only a few years.'

Edwin nodded quickly, starting to think more clearly now. 'And she knows her stuff.'

Perpetua coughed. 'He means I know what I'm talking about.'

Mersium took a deep breath. 'I think, Sire, that for now the less pressing question of the relic should be put to one side. Several skeletons hidden on Hysterian soil should be investigated without delay.'

Edwin blinked hard. He didn't know which problem was worse. Trust his luck to travel to the same place three times just when there was a crisis. No . . . when there were *two*. He looked at Perpetua. 'What are we gonna do?'

Perpetua looked right back at him. 'Oh, I think you know the answer to that.'

'Are you saying,' Janus asked, 'that you are willing to stay and help us?'

Edwin looked at the ground. Of course Perpetua was right. 'Yeah,' he said. 'Could you use a stunt double for the heir to the throne again?' He suddenly looked around. 'Hang on. Where *is* Auvlin?'

'He is away from the castle,' Janus replied. 'He will be with us this evening. And in answer to your first question, I do not know if we will need you to play Auvlin again.' He put his head to one side. 'If not, would you be disappointed?'

Edwin thought for a few seconds. 'A bit. But, to be

honest, Your Majesty, it's just nice being back here with you. Full stop.'

Perpetua put her finger in the air. 'He means *and that is all.*'

Janus's eyes glinted. 'I think I knew what he meant.' He took a few steps to Edwin and put his arm around his shoulder. 'Tomorrow I would like you to show me on a map where you and Perpetua found these bodies. You must rest for what is left of today and tonight you should reacquaint yourselves with my son.' He looked back at the relic nestling in its box, then handed it to Edwin. 'I think you should keep this for the time being.'

Edwin hesitated. 'Why, your Majesty?'

'The Queen's spirit guide spoke to you, and only you . . . he may wish to appear to you again.'

CHAPTER FIVE

EDWIN COULDN'T MAKE OUT WHERE he was. There was a glimmer of light in the distance, but all around him was shrouded in shadow. Ollie ran past him, carrying a football. Edwin opened his mouth to call him back, but his tongue was lifeless. He turned and a face sprang from the darkness. A savage expression with staring eyes. It snarled, exposing blackened teeth. There was a swish of a sword. Edwin edged back. He felt himself fall, the face fell after him . . .

'Wake up! Edwin . . . wake up!'

Edwin sat up, almost breathless. He looked at Perpetua. They were sitting on her bed.

'I was dreaming,' he said, almost to himself. 'It was a

dream . . .'

'You were twitching away for ages,' Perpetua said. She stood up and put her hands on her hips. 'Then you started giving these awful strangled moans. What were you dreaming about?'

Edwin swallowed. 'The Umbrian clones. The ones in the army.' He wiped a patch of sweat from his forehead. 'One was after Ollie . . . then it went for me, too.'

'Ugh! That's not a dream. That's a *nightmare.*'

Edwin swung his legs over the side of the bed. 'Tell me about it.' He looked around the room. There were clothes everywhere. 'What are you doing?'

Perpetua picked up a dark green dress and held it to her in front of a mirror. 'I'm looking at the clothes they've given me,' she said sourly. She turned from side to side and peered at her reflection as if she'd suddenly aged by 500 years.

Edwin looked at the mirror too. 'What's wrong with it?' he said.

Perpetua waived the long sleeves around her head. 'This was too big the last time I wore it. And it's *still* too big.'

Edwin rubbed his eyes. 'Right. So the real problem is that you haven't grown much.'

Perpetua stood bolt upright. 'No. It isn't that at all! Like any normal person I just want to wear something that fits. I'd be a laughing stock at school.'

'I could be wrong,' Edwin replied flatly, 'but I don't

think anyone at Templeton Grove Comp is gonna see you in that. You can't have everything,' he said, getting to his feet. 'You got all the right genes for your outsize brain, but you might have come up short in the growing stakes.' He guffawed. 'Ha! Ha! Come up short . . .'

'No pun intended, I take it,' Perpetua replied, trying not to smile. 'You're not clever enough! So,' she added, throwing the dress to one side. 'It looks as if things here are getting interesting.'

Edwin nodded. 'The bones in the cave – d'you reckon it's the Umbrians?'

'I think there's a very good chance they're involved,' Perpetua replied. 'The Hysterians aren't the sort of people to dump dead bodies in a cave and leave them to rot.'

'Well if you're right and the bones have only been there a few years, it could mean the bodies were put in the cave around the time we first came to Hysteria.'

'Yes, that had occurred to me.' Perpetua sat down. 'I suppose the first thing to do would be to find out who these people were. And where they came from.'

'Would they be Hysterian, though?' Edwin asked. 'If seven people had gone missing at the same time in the last few years, someone here would have made the connection when we told them what we found, wouldn't they?'

Perpetua nodded. 'I think we're probably looking at people from another part of the territories. And several people dying at once . . . I do wonder if it was some sort of ritual.'

'That sounds very Umbrian,' Edwin replied hesitantly 'Are you sure you want to stay and help Janus? We know what some of the Umbrians get up to – Shadow Magic, transformation of people, cloning. It's pretty scary.'

'I want to stay, I mean, if you do?'

Edwin sat up. 'Yeah, but it's different for me. I've played the part of Janus's son twice now, and I almost feel like he *is* my dad. My dad when I'm in Hysteria, I mean.'

Perpetua smiled. 'You feel a lot of loyalty to him, don't you? I do too, of course, but you two have a special bond. You know, it sounds like you won't need to impersonate Auvlin this time . . .'

'Yeah,' Edwin replied thoughtfully. 'But maybe it'll be good just being me. No formal dinners, nothing new to swot up on before I take his place.'

'Well I think that's a shame – I really enjoyed Ollwin's lessons.' Perpetua reached across to the pile of clothes belonging to Edwin, looking as if she were trying to hide a smirk. 'But one thing won't change – you're still going to have to wear tights!'

As Edwin walked with Perpetua towards the Great Hall he yanked at his backside. 'Why . . . won't . . . these . . . blimmin' . . . things . . . stay . . . up,' he growled.

At times like this, he thanked his lucky stars he wasn't a girl. What did they do in winter, having to wear these horrible things day after day? They itched. They itched *bad*. Edwin didn't care how warm they were – he'd rather let the icy north wind rattle around his knees on the walk to school.

Perpetua looked at Edwin and giggled. 'I bet you haven't put them on properly,' she said. 'They're all creased up around your ankles! Is there *anything* you can figure out for yourself?'

'Are you offering to teach me how to put on tights?' Edwin said.

Perpetua stared straight at him. 'If you think I'm going anywhere near your legs, you have another thing coming.'

They arrived at the entrance to the hall and the guards either side bowed their heads as Edwin and Perpetua passed through. They were the last to arrive. Everyone they had met earlier was sitting around the huge table, plus two more young men. Bellwin introduced one of them as his apprentice Delius and, just as Janus has promised, Auvlin was there too. When he saw Edwin and Perpetua walk into the room, he rose from his seat and rushed over to meet them.

'Edwin!' he said, offering his hand. 'You look just as I did two or three years ago.'

This made Edwin feel great. Auvlin was tall and his ordinary features had matured into what was quite a handsome face. Auvlin smiled at Perpetua then gave her a kiss. She coughed and walked quickly to an empty seat. Edwin sat next to her with Auvlin on the other side.

'How are you, Auvlin?' Edwin said.

'I am well, thank you. I am examined regularly to make sure that my recovery has been sustained. But after what has happened in the last two years I am just glad to be here in Emporium Castle.'

Edwin smiled. 'So, you got back into life at court all right, then?'

'Oh, yes. I have been very busy – along with my usual studies I have also been meeting prospective brides.'

Edwin's eyes widened. He remembered a very long afternoon two years ago, looking at endless portraits of foreign princesses. At least he hadn't had to *marry* anyone.

'Gosh!' Perpetua said. 'That must be a bit worrying. I mean, you're only seventeen, aren't you?'

'Yes,' Auvlin replied. 'But I have told my father I do not plan to marry for at least five years.'

Edwin raised his eyebrows. The only things he wanted to be doing at twenty-two were surfing professionally, watching lots of football and finding out what beer tasted like. And of course there would be girls, too.

'Are you allowed to go out with any of these princesses first?' he asked quietly.

Auvlin looked puzzled. 'What do you mean, Edwin?'

Perpetua scraped her chair a bit closer. 'He means are you allowed to go out on dates?'

Edwin frowned and imagined travelling on a piece of giant dried fruit. 'A date,' he said, 'is when two people, usually young ones as the older ones are all married, go out and spend time together. They might, er, go and have a drink.'

'A drink?' Auvlin repeated slowly. 'What do they drink from?'

Perpetua cleared her throat. 'When he says drink, it's usually a particular sort of drink called beer. It's a bit like your wine – it makes people very silly and gives them a very bad head the next morning.'

Auvlin didn't look any the wiser, but Perpetua carried on.

'People gather together and pay quite a lot of money to drink beer in special houses.'

Edwin nodded. 'And when you're going out with someone you also do stuff like . . .' He faltered, wishing he hadn't started this. '. . . like snogging,' he whispered.

'That's kissing, but with a bit more urgency,' said Perpetua. Then she went bright red.

Edwin cringed. 'Shall we talk about something else?'

'Yes!' Perpetua hissed.

Auvlin looked slightly relieved. 'My father is very grateful that you have brought my mother's relic back to Hysteria. He told me that you have seen my mother's spirit guide. He is so puzzled why it has only appeared to you. But I understand you are going to stay here to help discover the story behind those bodies.'

'Yep,' Edwin said. 'We're well up for it!'

'That means we really want to,' Perpetua added.

At that moment Janus stood up, and everyone fell quiet. He looked at all those gathered before he started to speak.

'My friends,' he said firmly. 'This is a day of conflicting emotions. First, our dear Edwin and Perpetua return to Hysteria with a long-lost keepsake belonging to my wife. Their presence does my heart good, and I know that all of you are happy to see them.'

Edwin glanced at Lorius. He was looking down his nose at the table.

'But, as you already know, they have discovered several bodies, seemingly hidden on Hysterian soil. Tomorrow morning Primus, Mersium and I will go with the King's Guard to the cave where they were found. We will bring the bodies back to Emporium Castle and begin investigations.'

'Ooh!' Perpetua cried. 'Just like forensics!'

Lorius threaded his fingers and shook his head. 'We have no such science here,' he sneered. 'You forget where you are, Perpetua.'

She looked down, but muttered to herself, 'It *still* involves the examination of bodies.'

Janus cleared his throat. 'It is time to eat, so further talk of this would not be fit.' He picked up a goblet and raised it. 'For now, we welcome our friends back to Hysteria. To Edwin, and Perpetua!'

It was the middle of the next morning. The King and his companions had left for the Inigo Forest very early and Auvlin was busy, so Edwin and Perpetua had taken the chance to catch up with Ollwin and Bellwin while they waited in the throne room. After an hour Edwin sat next to the throne to watch the misty glow of the vortex. Bellwin was telling Perpetua how he'd been getting on as a Full Wizard.

'. . . then I reversed the spell, and my mother's ears went back perfectly into place. She had been slightly worried before it was cast, but I assured her the process had worked well on the gatekeeper's dog.'

Perpetua bit her lip. 'And now you've got your own apprentice?'

'Yes,' Bellwin replied, cheering up. 'There is so much I can teach him.'

'My boy,' Ollwin said, 'you talk as if you yourself have nothing left to learn. I am still learning, and I have been a Full Wizard for over forty years.'

There was the sound of voices, and everyone turned to the Throne Room entrance. Two soldiers entered carrying large cloth sacks, followed by the King and the party that had gone to the forest.

'Put the sacks in the middle of the floor,' Janus

instructed. The soldiers did as they were told then stepped back, leaving everyone to gather around the bundles. Ollwin was the first to walk forward. He opened the top of one sack and looked inside. Reaching in slowly, he drew out a very long bone.

'From the upper leg,' he murmured.

'That's the femur,' Perpetua whispered into Edwin's ear.

Ollwin peered into the sack again and took out another bone. 'From the lower leg.'

'That's the tibia.'

Ollwin reached out for a third bone. 'From the shoulder area.'

'And that's—'

'I don't care,' whispered Edwin.

Bellwin touched Perpetua's arm. 'You can teach *me* all your terms for the human body, Perpetua,' he said. 'I am always willing to learn.'

'That's a deal,' Perpetua replied, shooting a snotty look at Edwin. 'At least *some* young men have enquiring minds.'

Mersium stepped forward and helped Ollwin take all the remains from the two sacks. They examined them together for a few minutes, then Ollwin held up his hands. 'It is impossible to tell who these people are just by looking at their skeletons.'

'Then we did right to bring them to Emporium Castle,' Mersium said. 'We can do our best to find out who they are and why they were in the cave.'

Ollwin asked the two soldiers to return the bones to the sacks, and they began to gently stack them on top of one another.

Janus shook his head. 'I have seen many bodies in battle, Ollwin, and the feeling is never any easier. I would have preferred the bodies to be carried individually, but the specimens were piled around the cave floor. Not a fitting end for any human being, no matter which land they come from.'

'Indeed, Sire,' Ollwin replied. 'Were there any remains of clothes in the cave?'

'*We* didn't see any,' Perpetua said quickly before Janus could even open his mouth. She looked at the king. 'But we didn't look for that long. Was there anything there this morning?'

'We did not notice anything else, Perpetua.'

All the remains were gathered up, and Ollwin looked carefully over the stone flags. 'In the cave, was there any sign of blood?'

'We did not see any,' Mersium replied.

'So they may have died somewhere else.'

'Or been killed somewhere else,' Primus said firmly.

'Yes, quite so,' Ollwin agreed.

'At home, we'd probably be able to tell whether they were murdered or died of natural causes,' Perpetua said. 'It's a shame you don't have forensics here.'

'We have coped very well so far without such things,'

Ollwin replied. 'We will find a solution to the problem, Perpetua.' He turned to the king. 'Can I have the remains taken to my chambers for two or three days, Sire? I am sure Lorius would like to join me in their examination.'

Lorius nodded. 'Of course, Ollwin. Hysterian science may be limited, but I too will attempt a conclusion.'

Janus crossed his arms and sighed. 'Yes, my lords. Do whatever you think is necessary.' He looked at the soldiers. 'Take the sacks to Master Ollwin's chambers. Be very careful with them.'

Edwin could see a nerve flicker in the king's cheek. It was the look of worry he'd seen many times before.

The sacks were picked up and carried from the throne room. Edwin could hear the contents grating together in a dry rattle.

'I don't have a good feeling about this,' he said to Bellwin.

The young wizard looked back at Edwin with a hesitant stare. 'Me neither, my friend.'

CHAPTER SIX

JANUS AND HIS COURT WERE preoccupied with the question of the bodies, so for the moment the mystery of the relic was put to one side. As well as helping wherever they could, Edwin and Perpetua spent the next few days getting back into the swing of Emporium Castle. As Perpetua didn't know the castle like Edwin did, he gave her the grand tour and dug out one of the old maps that he'd drawn for her. She spent a day revising Hysterian history, discovering happily that she hadn't forgotten anything, while Edwin brushed up on his swordsmanship with Primus. On their third morning in Hysteria, Bellwin came to find them at breakfast.

'Good morning!' he chimed as he entered the

otherwise empty dining hall. 'How are my two earthly friends today?'

Edwin was inspecting a sprinkling of large grey flakes on his plate, but he looked up with a smile. 'Crikey, Bellwin. You sound chirpy!'

'He means you seem very happy,' Perpetua said. 'And I must say he's right.'

'Oh, yes. I am very happy this morning,' Bellwin replied. 'I begin training Delius today.'

Edwin's eyes lit up. 'Wicked!'

Perpetua looked at Bellwin. It seemed he remembered her translation from before.

'Can we come and watch?' Edwin asked.

Bellwin looked a little taken aback. 'If you would like to,' he said hesitantly.

'Yeah!' said Edwin. 'Wouldn't miss it for the world.'

'Only if you really don't mind,' Perpetua said. 'I'm sure you'll be nervous enough as it is.'

'No. No, no. What do I have to be nervous about?' Bellwin replied, nervously. 'I . . . I am a Full Wizard of two years standing. I complete my tasks with absolute competence and efficiency.' He swallowed. 'Ask my mother – her ears went back in just the right place.'

Perpetua grimaced. 'Yes. You'll be fine. No problem at all.'

'Of course I will, dear friend. But I must do some more preparation.' Bellwin's fingers wrestled around each other.

'What's the latest on the bones?' Edwin asked.

'Lorius, Ollwin and some other wizard masters will be working on the identification of the skeletons again today,' said Bellwin. 'They have not yet come to any conclusions.'

Perpetua sighed. 'It's a shame I can't just pop home with one or two of the remains and take them straight to the police . . . forensics would find an answer in no time.'

Edwin looked at Perpetua as if she were completely bonkers. 'Yeah right – you waltz into Templeton Grove Police Station and say "these bones are from a parallel world. They might have something to do with these people called the Umbrians who do something called Shadow Magic. Can you sort it, please?" They'd put you in the first available straight jacket.' Then he frowned. 'And don't they have to compare DNA to something else, to tell if it's the right thing they're looking for? If you know what I mean.'

Perpetua's eyes were wide. 'Goodness, Edwin – I know exactly what you mean. You are actually *right*.' She quickly shook her head. 'But I'm only thinking out loud.'

'So, Bellwin,' Edwin said. 'Will Lorius and Ollwin just keep trying?'

Bellwin nodded firmly. 'Ollwin has said many times that as long as the spirit of Hereticus is alive then anything could be possible. Those people died in the cave two or three years ago – perhaps when Hereticus's spirit was present *within this castle*. This could all be connected. There may still be some threat to Hysteria from that awful time.' Bellwin crossed his arms. 'Of course, Janus would not hesitate to fight the threat, but first he has to be sure.'

Edwin raised his eyebrows. 'This is Hysteria,' he said flatly. 'If there's no danger then I'm a monkey's uncle.'

Bellwin looked quite alarmed and Perpetua jumped in. 'He's not a monkey's uncle – that's just a phrase we have at home to comment that something is very unlikely.'

'I see,' Bellwin said, sounding as if he didn't see at all. 'I actually came to ask how you found your breakfast. I helped the cooks with their preparation this morning. Were they successful?'

Edwin scraped his spoon around his plate and held it aloft. 'If you told them to try and make elephant dandruff, I think they pulled it off!'

'Ele-phant dand-ruff?' Bellwin repeated carefully. 'Is that a delicacy on your Earth by any chance?'

'Not exactly,' Edwin replied. 'What did you asked them to copy?'

Bellwin pointed a finger in the air. 'I remembered what you asked for on your very first morning in Hysteria two years ago. I asked them to copy *that*.'

Edwin narrowed his eyes, trying to think. It was an awfully long time ago . . .

'Got it!' he said suddenly. 'Cornflakes!'

'Yes!' Bellwin cried. 'It is exactly that. I am very pleased you liked it. The cooks will be delighted.'

'Yep!' said Edwin, forcing down another mouthful.

Bellwin clasped his hands. 'The day has started so very well. And I will interpret that as the best possible omen. Do come to see me begin my work with Delius this morning,' he added, now sounding quite enthusiastic. 'My earthly friends are always welcome!'

'Can't wait!' grinned Perpetua. 'I'm really looking forward to it!'

Bellwin smiled broadly and almost skipped out of the hall. Perpetua creased her nose and looked at Edwin.

'I didn't know elephants could get dandruff . . . ?'

Edwin and Perpetua ate what little was edible on their plates before they went to Bellwin's workroom.

'Hello,' said Delius brightly, stepping forward. He had very straight black hair and twinkly brown eyes. 'It was very nice to meet you last night.'

'Hello, Delius,' Edwin replied. 'How are you? Were you nervous about coming to the castle?'

Delius smiled. 'Oh, no. I have been here countless times to use the library.'

Perpetua shook his hand approvingly. 'And now you're training to be a wizard! Bellwin hasn't told us much about you.'

'There is not much to tell,' Delius replied cheerfully. 'I was expected to train as a wizard, so that is all I have ever thought about. My family has wizards going back fifteen generations. Three of them have been High Wizards, like Master Ollwin.'

Perpetua looked impressed. 'So you may go on to great things, Delius. My mother and father are both renowned chemists and I intend to follow entirely in their footsteps.'

It was Edwin's turn to translate. 'Chemistry is a science we have on Earth. It's all about elements and test tubes and mucking around with stinky powder, and it's very, very boring.'

'That may be your interpretation, Edwin, but chemistry is the basis of all life. Including *yours*. It's a little bit like magic, actually.' Perpetua smiled at Delius. 'Are you looking forward to learning from Bellwin?'

'Oh, yes. Although I do have a little knowledge already.' Delius clicked his fingers and shouted, 'On sera!' His waistcoat peeled itself off his body and levitated a metre from the floor.

Bellwin's eyes widened. 'How did you do that?' he said.

Delius clicked his fingers again and the waistcoat flew back on. 'It was a spell my father taught me when I was four. It is a very old set spell – to help children get dressed and undressed. Is your father a wizard, Master Bellwin?'

'No,' said Bellwin weakly. He crossed his arms over his stomach. 'He is a baker. But I have learnt from many fine wizards. Master Ollwin, of course. And Wizard Brolin from Meticulla. Have you heard of him?'

'Yes!' Delius said, his eyes wide. 'You have *met* Hildeguard Brolin?'

Bellwin nodded. He looked relieved to have finally impressed his apprentice. 'Wizard Brolin seems to know almost everything about magic.' He gave a meaningful look. 'Even Shadow Magic.'

Delius blinked. 'Does he? May I ask what he knows?'

Inevitably, Perpetua muscled her way in. 'Edwin, Bellwin and I visited Wizard Brolin in Meticulla last year, and what he told us was amazing. Are you aware that the Umbrians practise Shadow Magic and by doing so break Ancient Magical Law?'

'Yes, I am,' Delius said, fidgeting like an excited child.

Bellwin shook his head at Perpetua, as if he'd started something he really shouldn't have. But Perpetua crashed on like a driverless juggernaut.

'So Brolin told us that the punishment is the loss of vital elements from the blood, which leads to death. It would of course take some time, so the Umbrian Wizards get around it by drinking the blood of other humans, which gives them back the vital elements they need.'

'On Earth,' Edwin added, 'we call people who drink human blood "vampires".'

'That is fascinating,' Delius gasped. 'Where do they get the blood from?'

'That we don't know,' said Perpetua. 'But there are lots of wizards in Umbria who practise Shadow Magic, so they'll need a constant supply. I wonder if—'

Bellwin raised a hand. 'If Master Ollwin were here, he would say a discussion of consumption of human blood is not fit for the ears of an apprentice. Delius, you are here to learn about White Magic.' He started to stride manfully about the room. 'I think we will begin with something very easy. Something that Ollwin taught me when I first began my apprenticeship.' Bellwin stood thoughtfully in front of a bookshelf, rocking back and forth of his heels, hands clasped behind his back. 'Perhaps the Herbal charm.'

'Yes,' Delius replied, 'I have—'

'This way!' Bellwin interrupted.

Delius followed Bellwin to the other side of the room.

'Point at the glass jar and repeat after me,' Bellwin instructed. 'Herbarium recepticas!'

Delius looked at Bellwin. 'Herba*lium* recepti*cus*,' he said quietly.

Bellwin frowned. 'Yes . . . yes, carry on.'

Delius took a deep breath. 'Herbalium recepticus!' he shouted, pointing at the jar. A cloud of green smoke filled it then shrank back, leaving a bunch of bright green leaves sprouting from the bottom.

Bellwin's mouth fell open and he leaned in to have a closer look. 'By Janus,' he whispered. 'That is a very well grown herb. It is much bigger than . . .'

Edwin and Perpetua exchanged glances. It looked as if Bellwin would be the one learning from Delius.

Bellwin cleared his throat and straightened up. 'A very good effort, Delius,' he said grandly. 'But next time you should point your figure in a much straighter manner.'

Edwin smothered a giggle. Perpetua suddenly developed a terrible cough. 'Yes, well done, Delius,' she spluttered. 'You're obviously in very good hands.'

Bellwin gave a pained smile. 'Do you two have anything to do?' he said.

'We, er, thought we were gonna stay here for the day?' Edwin replied.

'I think Delius may prefer start his apprenticeship with just us two,' Bellwin said firmly.

Delius shook his head. 'But I—'

'Of course he does!' Perpetua leaped to her feet, grabbed Edwin's hand and pulled him towards the door. 'They need to start this sort of thing in *private*,' she said pointedly. 'No one wants spectators watching their every move on their very first day!'

'Bellwin looks like he's got a right one there – Delius is like the Hysterian version of you,' said Edwin as they headed away from Bellwin's workroom. 'What are we gonna do, then?'

'We can do some research on the thing that brought

us here: the Queen's relic,' Perpetua replied, ignoring his first comment. 'We've hardly found out anything about it!'

'But Mersium and everyone else agreed that should come later.'

Perpetua grabbed Edwin's arm. '*They* are investigating the bodies, why not make ourselves really useful and get a head start on something else?'

'Oh. OK,' Edwin said, taking one last glance back.

'Right,' Perpetua said bossily. 'We'll get the relic from your room, then we'll get down to business.'

'The library?' Edwin said flatly.

Perpetua smiled. 'You've got it in one.'

They reached the library in no time at all. Perpetua was always very disapproving about the state of the room, but Edwin knew she loved it. Apart from in the school laboratory, he'd never seen her look more at home.

'What this place needs is a proper librarian!' Perpetua said as she swept through the doors. 'Oh,' she said, stopping dead. 'It's looks as if it finally has one . . .'

Edwin scratched his head. The library was usually a monumental mess. But now the place was clean and all the shelves were neatly stacked.

Perpetua clapped her hands. 'That just makes our research much easier. Right! You get the pendant out, I'll look for *Ancient Relics of These Territories.*'

Edwin did as he was told and put the box containing the pendant on the table. He could hear Perpetua scurrying around. After a few minutes she made some distinctively impatient noises.

'I spoke too soon!' she wailed, stomping back to sit down. 'The book is *not* where it should be. It'll take me a month of Sundays to find it . . . How hard can it be to catalogue sensibly?'

Edwin narrowed his eyes. 'You know what, Perpetua,' he said slowly. 'Someone else might've borrowed it.'

Perpetua blinked. 'Yes, I suppose so. But who? And why?' She drummed her fingers on the table. 'I wonder if relics are mentioned in any of the other books.'

'There's only one way to find out and that's to read them all of 'em.' Edwin crossed his arms. 'But I'd quite like to get home before it's time for me to draw my pension.'

Perpetua scoffed. 'We simply need to be selective.' She stood up. 'You look for anything that might include text about the queen. I'll look for anything that might feature Ancient Relics.'

Edwin spent the next two hours doing what he considered to be the worst thing possible – looking through reference books. There were quite a lot that included text about the queen, but there was nothing in them that struck Edwin as any sort of clue.

'Crikey,' he said at one point, 'Janus married the queen five days after he met her. *Five days*! That's only the length of a cricket match.'

'But a lot more interesting,' said Perpetua. 'I am sure they were madly in love,' she added wistfully. 'Janus strikes me as the romantic type.'

Edwin cringed. He carried on reading. 'It says here that the queen was sure before they *even met* that they'd get married and be really happy together.' Edwin raised his eyebrows. 'So when Janus asked her to marry him after only a few hours, she said yes straight away. Bit risky, don't you think?'

'Well, she was right, wasn't she?' said Perpetua. 'Perhaps something from the spirit world had helped her see into the future.'

Edwin didn't look convinced. No one would catch *him* proposing to a girl after the time it took to watch two episodes of *Doctor Who*. 'It's bonkers,' he said firmly.

Perpetua skimmed the pages of the books much quicker than Edwin and already had a pile of six by her side when she suddenly stopped. 'This could take a lot longer than I thought.'

Edwin smirked. 'Getaway. I could've told you that *ages* ago.'

Perpetua crossed her arms sulkily. Then her gaze lowered to the box on the table and her eyes widened. 'Let's get the relic out!'

Edwin frowned. 'Looking at it again won't tell us anything new . . . '

'That's *not* what I'm saying.'

Edwin knew what Perpetua meant straight away. 'Seriously?' he said slowly. 'After everything I told you, you want me to pick it up?'

'Why not?' Perpetua replied lightly. 'It didn't *hurt you* before.'

'Oh, no! It just scared the pants off me!'

'I'm here, in the broad light of day.'

Edwin put his head in his hands. 'Do I *have* to?'

Perpetua raised her eyesbrows but didn't reply.

Edwin looked up. He couldn't believe he was about to say this. 'All right, I'll do it . . . but not for long.'

Perpetua sat up as Edwin prepared himself. He took a deep breath, extended his fingers slightly, then snatched the relic from the table. His hand warmed straight away and he dropped the pendant. It rolled a few centimetres then came to a stop. As before the air crackled and in less than a minute the hooded figure was standing beside the table, its body motionless but its stained lips moving rapidly. Once again its words were lost in a crackly hiss.

'Oh . . . goodness,' Perpetua gasped, edging back in her chair. 'I – I didn't expect . . .'

'Try to listen to what it says,' Edwin whispered, narrowing his eyes and concentrating on its lips.

But what happened next took them both by surprise.

The hooded figure began to move. It didn't walk, but its form seemed to blur through the air. It was moving slowly – towards Perpetua.

'What's it doing?' she yelped, springing to her feet.

As it moved closer, the hiss became deeper. Odd words jumped out of the jumble. Now the figure's hands stretched towards Perpetua. The face moved too, its form distorting like runny wet paint. Streams of grey touched Perpetua's skin and seemed to seep into it. She began to cry.

'Stop it, Edwin!' she screamed. 'Help me!'

Just as Edwin reached out for Perpetua, her voice faded. Her face and body disappeared into a blurry mess. Standing there just a few seconds later, where Perpetua had been, looking as solid and human as she had, was the ghost.

'Where's she gone?' Edwin blurted.

The figure began to walk around the table. Edwin tried to stand firm but felt himself inching back.

'tic . . . tic . . . tic . . .'

The figure jolted with the sound three times, then advanced on.

'The spirit . . .'

It was getting closer to Edwin and its hand rose to grasp the hood of his cloak.

'. . . the spirit finds . . .'

The hood was about to be pulled back.

'. . . the spirit finds . . . tic . . . tic . . . tic . . .'

There was a loud buzz. A crackle of static flew to Edwin's outstretched hand.

'. . . the spirit *finds* . . . tic . . . tic . . . tic . . .'

The hood was pulled back a few inches. The figure's lips were in full light, discoloured still, but darker than before – almost purple. The raised hand began to shake. The lips began to tremble. The mouth contorted. A rattling gasp crept out.

'. . . tic . . . tic . . . tic . . . NO!'

The solid form crackled into 2D, like an image on a screen. It began to shrink and turn in on itself, before expanding in a split second. And there, standing in front of Edwin, white and breathless, was Perpetua.

CHAPTER SEVEN

EDWIN GRABBED PERPETUA'S SHOULDERS. SHE was shaking violently as he sat her down.

'Are you all right?'

'It was like it was . . . possessing me,' Perpetua whispered, as tears rolled down her cheeks. 'It made me move. I felt it inside my head. It's terrified . . . there's something scaring it and there's something it needs to do.' She closed her eyes. 'I felt it speak . . . its words were in my mouth – "The spirit finds . . ." Did you hear it?'

'Yeah.' Edwin put his arm around Perpetua's shoulder. 'Loud and clear.'

'What does it mean?' Perpetua leaned into Edwin,

almost clinging to him. She was still shaking. 'What if he's trying to tell us something? Something really important.' She suddenly sat up and took a deep breath. 'I need to be rational. "The spirit finds . . ." Maybe it was talking about me. *It* found *me*.' She shook her head. 'That's all I can think of. So we've been through all that and we're no further forward.'

Edwin didn't really care, he just wanted to make sure his friend was all right. 'It doesn't matter,' he said gently. 'Like you said, we haven't learnt anything new, so we'll tell Janus what happened and we'll try to forget about it.'

Edwin helped Perpetua to her feet and she turned, popped the relic back in the box and handed it to him. As Edwin walked Perpetua to her room he knew one thing for certain – he wouldn't be picking up that stupid thing again.

Edwin and Perpetua told Janus and Ollwin what had happened and they both came to the same conclusion as Perpetua: the spirit had found *her*. Edwin had made it clear he didn't want to handle the relic a third time, so Janus didn't ask to see the spirit for himself.

'The vision has appeared to you and only to you,' the king said. 'It may sound strange, my boy, but it almost seems as if the relic *belongs* with you. Still, I will keep it by my side if you would rather not have it in your possession.' Edwin nodded with relief.

Perpetua was very shaken by what had happened, but when anyone tried to make her feel better she just told them to stop fussing. She seemed to concentrate all her thoughts back on the bodies, not even mentioning the relic the next day. Edwin had a feeling Perpetua was planning something and that evening she made an announcement.

'I think we should go back to the cave,' she said to Edwin matter-of-factly. 'There might be something that Janus and the others missed and we need to be sure the place has been scoured thoroughly.'

'OK,' Edwin replied, unable to think of better plan. 'I'll tell Janus – just to check it out with him.'

'I'd rather you didn't,' Perpetua said quickly.

Edwin frowned. 'Why?'

'Janus might not like me suggesting he and his soldiers didn't search the cave properly,' Perpetua replied. 'And I'm *dying* to do something scientifically useful.'

Edwin agreed and quite early the next morning they were ready. They told Janus they wanted to go out riding and he'd insisted that a few of the King's Guard go with them. The castle gates were about to be opened when Bellwin appeared out of nowhere and scurried over the cobbles. Delius was following a little way behind.

'I saw you from the tower,' Bellwin said breathlessly. 'Wherever you are going, can we come with you?'

'Er . . . haven't you got an apprentice to teach?' said Edwin.

Bellwin shook his head. 'We decided we should have a break from lessons.' He looked at Delius as he stood beside him. 'Yesterday was very tiring, and I think Delius will need a short period of recuperation.'

'But I am perfectly well,' Delius said. 'I do not feel—'

'But you *look* so tired,' Bellwin insisted. 'And I am sure it will do us good to get some exercise and fresh air.' He looked from Edwin to Perpetua. His expression was almost desperate.

'Yeah, course you can come,' said Edwin in a low voice. 'We've told Janus we're going riding, but we're gonna go back to the cave . . . where the skeletons were.'

'Oh,' Bellwin said, looking surprised. 'Well, Delius and I would like to come along.'

Edwin smiled. 'Investigating Hysterian mysteries just wouldn't be the same without you, Bellwin. Are you ready to go now?'

'Yes, quite ready. Delius is carrying some food and water.'

The gates to the castle swung back, and they rode a little way before Edwin turned to Bellwin again. 'So, how did the first day go?'

Bellwin coughed. 'It was a great success, Edwin. I learned – I mean *Delius* learned so much in such a short time.'

'Excellent!' said Perpetua.

'Bellwin is so kind,' Delius said slowly, as if he were trying to think of something to say. 'So kind. And so . . . *kind*.'

Edwin nodded firmly. 'Yes,' he agreed. 'He is very, *very* kind.'

There was a long silence.

'I am receiving extra tuition from my father,' Delius added suddenly. 'Just in case . . . er, I . . .'

Edwin glanced at Bellwin, who looked a little crestfallen. 'Well, that's a good thing. I mean . . . it's a good thing that your father is also kind enough to give you some extra lessons. Even if you *don't* need them.'

Bellwin coughed. He looked as if he wanted to change the subject. 'Shall we tell Delius the background to our trip? He knows nothing of what we found.'

'Yeah, course,' Edwin replied. 'Let me—'

But Perpetua took over. 'Well,' she started. 'This is our third trip to Hysteria and when we arrived *this* time . . .'

Edwin concluded that Delius had a massive capacity for being talked at. The whole time Perpetua had chattered on he'd looked focused and interested, even saying 'yes' and 'I see' in all the right places. If it'd been Edwin, he would have switched off *ages* ago.

As the horses approached the part of the forest surrounding the cave, Perpetua finally stopped. Edwin was careful to make sure that no one else was around and then he led the way through the densely packed trees. He wasn't at all worried this time – Janus, Mersium and Primus had been in the cave and the bones weren't even there now. Within a minute all four of them were standing outside the entrance, staring in.

'I will summon some light,' Bellwin said and then muttered, 'Illuminum!' A small sphere suddenly appeared and started to glow. It wasn't very bright, but it was enough to take into the cave.

Edwin asked the soldiers to stay outside and glanced around at everyone else. 'Come on, then,' he said. 'Let's get going.'

They crept forward, Edwin and Perpetua leading the way. The cave was much less scary when it was lit up. The walls glowed a pretty yellow and now they could see much further inside.

'The bones were around here,' Perpetua said, kneeling down. She took her glasses from her pocket and started to look closely at the ground, running her hands over the dust and dirt. 'I can't see anything but stones and bits of grass and leaves,' she muttered after a few minutes.

'So what are we looking for?' Delius asked.

Edwin raised his eyebrows. That was a good question. Why hadn't he asked it?

'Traces of cloth,' said Perpetua. 'Buttons, bits of paper, blood stains . . . anything!'

Edwin, Bellwin and Delius got to their knees, each taking a section of ground a few metres apart. Edwin scoured what was in front of him, but didn't find a thing. The only thing of any interest came when a large brown spider scuttled across his hand.

'Any luck, anyone?' Edwin asked eventually.

Bellwin slumped back on his knees. 'Nothing so far,' he replied. He glanced around. 'Is there anywhere else in the cave we should look?'

Perpetua got to her feet. 'There could be something on the walls, or on the rocks.' She strode to a huge boulder and tried to peer beneath it. 'I don't suppose anything has managed to find its way under there . . .'

Edwin stood up and crossed his arms. He was pretty sure that if anything was to be found, Mersium, Primus and Janus would have done so already. Then something caught Edwin's eye. In the moderate light he could just make out a line of holes in the cave wall. They were all at about knee height and a regular distance apart. He walked to the wall and squatted down, running his fingers over the holes. They all looked to be about the same size – he could fit the tip of his little finger in the opening of the nearest. He moved his hand along, doing the same to each one, and then he stopped. *This* one had something in it.

'Look at this,' he said quickly to the others. Everyone got to their feet and stood back.

'A line of holes in the cave wall,' Edwin explained. 'They're all empty except this one – it's got something in it that *just* sticks out.'

Perpetua scurried over to join Edwin. She ran her fingers around the shape that was proud of the rock. 'That feels like metal to me.' She took a few steps back.

'How many holes are there?' said Delius enthusiastically. 'That may help us.'

'Good idea!' Edwin strode to the lighter end of the cave and started to count. 'One . . . two . . . three . . . four . . .' He heard Perpetua mutter something and looked up – she was mouthing the numbers too. Edwin rolled his eyes as he hopped over a rock. 'Fourteen . . . fifteen . . . er, sixteen.' Edwin stopped. 'I can't see any more. Could you turn that orb thing up a bit, Bellwin?'

Bellwin hesitated. He didn't seem too sure. 'Why not let Delius attempt the spell,' he said. 'Perhaps the orbs from us both can merge to form something much brighter? '

'Perfect!' Edwin said. He crossed his arms and waited.

Bellwin looked at Delius. 'Now,' he said. 'You should say the word firmly . . .'

Suddenly, Edwin heard a faint chink from somewhere. It sounded metallic. He turned his head towards the darkness. But no, it must have come from the men outside.

'Emphasise the first two syllables . . . '

There was the sound of a gasping breath.

'Your focus must be complete . . .'

And a rasping as it exhaled.

'Illuminum!'

A second sphere appeared and streaked towards the first. They merged in a burst of yellow and the cave was flooded with light. For a split second Edwin saw something at the back of the cave, but instinct made him cover his eyes from the light. He blinked and lowered his hand. Someone was running towards him . . .

'Edwin!' Perpetua screamed.

He focused on a very tall man. Tall and thin, with chains hanging from his wasted wrists. His eyes were wide, bulging from sunken sockets. The mouth gaped into a snarl, thick saliva seeping from the side.

Within a few seconds the man reached Edwin, who ducked and leaped to his left. The man kept going and hit the wall, his head bouncing off the rock. He reeled back, stood dazed for a few seconds then turned.

As Edwin scrambled to his feet, Bellwin rushed forward and grabbed the man's arm. Barely glancing around, the man shrugged off Bellwin like a child and returned his focus to Edwin, glare locked in place.

Perpetua lunged towards the clone, but Bellwin grabbed her ankle and she fell into the dust.

'No!' Bellwin shouted. 'He'll hurt you. HELP!' he screamed 'HELP!'

'Let go!' Perpetua yelled. 'Let me go!'

Edwin was scrambling to get away, but the man was too fast. The man's lips clamped together and he sniffed. Edwin could hear the rasp of sputum in his throat, could smell the stench of his breath. Then the mouth gaped again, this time wider, as if the man was hungry. Liquid spilled through rotten teeth and down his chin. Edwin felt his stomach churn.

A rock flew through the air. It hit the man's temple and bounced to the ground. The man faltered for a few seconds and Edwin grabbed the chance to get away. He threw himself towards the back of the cave, his legs shaking. He was heading towards two tunnels, both of which led to darkness. Edwin could hear the man behind him and the sound of other footsteps. He lurched into the left hand tunnel, desperately hoping his friends were behind him.

But had they seen which tunnel he'd gone into? Edwin swallowed against his dry tongue. He couldn't see a thing. He put his hands out in front of him and could feel them trembling. He didn't even know what was in there. Could there be another one of those things crouching in the darkness? But he couldn't just stand there, waiting, like bait in a trap.

'Where are you, Edwin?' Perpetua's frantic words echoed up the tunnel.

Edwin opened his mouth, but his throat was frozen. Should he call out? Run back?

Something hit him. He fell to the ground, a weight bearing down on his legs. A foul smell hit Edwin again. He heard jaws snap together; saliva wash around itself. The man was shaking too, as he dragged himself up Edwin's body, getting closer and closer to his head . . .

'HELP!' Edwin wrestled the word from his mouth. He tried to pull himself away, reaching out his fingers for something to hold on to. All he could feel was loose shale and dirt. Edwin heard the man lunging forward and put up his hands. They pressed against the man's torso. The man put his hands on Edwin's face and fingers dug into Edwin's cheeks. Edwin strained to keep the man's head away, turning desperately from the stench of his breath. His arms began to fail him. His muscles were burning. He couldn't keep this up . . .

Suddenly, the man stopped moving. There was a long strangled sigh, a rush of gravelly breath, then nothing. Edwin used all his strength to push the man to one side. He scrambled to his feet and lurched towards the light.

'I'm here,' he said weakly, wiping his mouth with his sleeve. 'I'm here . . .'

Bellwin, Perpetua and the soldiers came rushing out of the other tunnel.

'Oh my God!' Perpetua gasped. 'Are you okay? Where's the man?'

'In there,' Edwin replied. 'I think there's something wrong with him.'

Bellwin and the soldiers crept to the entrance to the other tunnel. The orb followed them, with Perpetua in tow.

'He looks dead,' Perpetua whispered, squinting into the light. 'Look at him – he's just skin and bone.' She turned back to Edwin. 'What happened in there?'

Edwin leaned back against the wall, his limbs still shaking. 'I think he was trying to get to my head. Then he stopped moving and he made some funny sounds. There was a really loud breath,' He blinked hard. 'Then I managed to get out.'

'And you didn't feel him move again?'

Edwin shook his head and then hesitated for a moment. 'Do you think he *is* dead, Perpetua?'

'Yes. He may have had a heart attack.'

All six of them took a few careful steps closer. The man lay on its front with its head to one side; a pool of green mucus had collected by his mouth.

'He looks pretty dead to me,' Edwin said hopefully. He got his first proper look at the man's face and his mouth slowly dropped. Why hadn't he recognised it before? 'You know what this is, don't you?' he said.

Perpetua had gone very quiet. She looked at Edwin and nodded. 'It's an Umbrian clone.'

Bellwin gasped, 'By Janus!' He put his arms out to hold Edwin and Perpetua back. 'We must be careful,' he gabbled. 'These creatures will fight while there is any breath left in their body!'

They approached the clone cautiously and Perpetua and Edwin knelt down. The two Hysterian soldiers were close by their sides. 'I don't want to touch him,' Perpetua grimaced. 'But I think I'm going to have to.'

Perpetua reached out for the clone's wrist. Edwin

could see her hand tremble and she had to steady it with the other as she rested her fingers on the clone's skin. Her expression was steely for a few seconds.

'He *is* dead,' Perpetua squeaked, whipping her hand away. She lunged to her feet and scuttled back out of the tunnel. 'God! His flesh felt awful!'

Edwin looked to the back of the tunnel. It was a closed end. 'Is the other tunnel safe?' he asked, getting up.

'Yes, there is nothing in there,' Bellwin replied. He put a hand on Edwin's shoulder. 'Are you able to ride back to the castle, my friend?'

'Yeah, I'm OK.' But Edwin leaned on Bellwin as they walked out of the tunnel. They found Perpetua with her hands on her hips staring at the wall. 'You know what these holes are, don't you?' she said.

Everyone looked blank.

'No,' Edwin replied.

'They've been used to hold chains. Can you see how many pairs there are? It's eight. The seven bodies that we found . . . and *him*.' She nodded into darkness.

Edwin blinked. 'So all the bones we found here were from Umbrian clones?'

'Correct. They were obviously kept prisoner in here and after they'd died – or been killed – the shackles were removed from their bodies and the chains taken away.' Perpetua folded her arms. 'Although they left behind that bit of the metal you found.'

Bellwin scratched his head. 'These clones were not

held prisoner by Hysterians, surely?'

'You wouldn't think so,' Edwin replied. 'Janus has got a whacking great castle for that.'

'I wonder why there is one Umbrian left?' Delius piped up. 'And why he did not leave?'

'Good questions,' Edwin said. 'But I don't have a clue about the answers.'

Everyone fell silent. Edwin felt like what had just happened was almost too much to take in.

'We should get back – quickly,' Perpetua said eventually. 'Janus needs to know what's gone on here.'

Nobody spoke. They all knew Perpetua was right. And as they rode back to Emporium Castle, Edwin couldn't help but think that they might be in trouble.

'EDWIN Spencer! PERPETUA Allbright! Every time you venture out on your own you seem to come into harm's way.'

Edwin grimaced. Janus didn't look very pleased, and as Edwin stood in the courtyard, looking down at his shoes, he felt as if he was in the Headmaster's office. But he hoped that what they'd found out might let them off the hook.

'A year ago you went to Meticulla without even telling me and with only a novice wizard for protection.'

Now it was Bellwin's turn to look at his shoes.

The King sighed. 'But on that occasion you *also* came

across information that was invaluable in our fight against the Umbrians.'

Ollwin coughed. 'It is obvious that the creature living in the cave *was* a clone, but something puzzles me. If the *rest* of the bodies in the cave were clones, all the bones would surely be of the same proportions. But they are not.'

Perpetua folded her arms, then looked up. 'Where are the bones?' she asked.

'They are all laid out in a room adjoining my chambers,' Ollwin replied.

'I'd like to have a look at them, if that's OK?'

It was clear to Edwin that everyone knew how clever Perpetua was, as nobody had raised an eyebrow when she'd asked to see the remains. In fact, everyone followed her to Ollwin's chambers, all keen to watch her look at them.

Perpetua dived straight in. She examined the femurs first – instructing everybody, even if they already knew, that these were the longest bones in the human body. She laid them all side by side in descending length order.

'Hmmm,' she muttered after studying them for a few minutes. 'There's a definite difference in length between some of them. What I need to find,' she added, as if to herself, 'is the same anomaly in all of them ...'

Edwin glanced at Bellwin, but his friend looked just as confused as he did.

Perpetua went to the group of skulls. She pushed her glasses up her nose and examined one very carefully. 'Oh, let's try that,' she said. She put the first one down and picked up a second. 'Ah! It's here!' She did the same with the third and the fourth and so on, until she'd studied each of the seven skulls.

'Ollwin,' Perpetua said grandly. 'I can confirm that these remains are indeed clones of one original.'

The wizard looked slightly hesitant. 'But how can you tell, my dear?' he said carefully.

'I knew you'd ask me that!' Perpetua strode over to Ollwin and held up the smallest skull. 'Can you see this?' she said, pointing to a small nodule of bone on the jaw. 'This irregularity of the mandible is present in each and every one of these skulls. That can only mean that these humans were clones. The limb bones are slightly different sizes because—'

'How stupid of me,' said Ollwin, as if something had suddenly dawned on him. 'They are different sizes because not all of the clones were fully grown.'

Perpetua smiled. 'Exactly. None of the remains are from younger children, but there are certainly some of older teenagers – sixteen, seventeen, I'd say.'

Edwin blinked. He had to hand it to Perpetua: she knew more stuff than any other kid he'd ever met. She was even smarter than his sisters.

'This is not good news,' said Janus. 'I had hoped the remains were nothing to do with Umbria. But they are, and it must be dealt with.' He put his hands behind his back. 'Why would Umbrian soldiers be chained in a cave on Hysterian soil? Does that mean they had been kept prisoner by Hysterians?'

Primus frowned. 'I do not think that would be the case, Sire. What use would a citizen of this kingdom have for such creatures?'

'Too right,' Edwin said weakly. 'I wouldn't wanna go near one if I didn't have to.'

'Just think how badly the Umbrians treated their own when transforming young men to look like Auvlin,' Primus continued. 'I would pledge my life that this is *their* work.'

'But to our knowledge the Umbrians use the clones in their army,' Janus replied. 'Why would they be imprisoned here, on Hysterian soil?'

'*To our knowledge,*' Edwin repeated. 'That hits the nail on the head!'

'That means it's the crux of the matter,' Perpetua added quickly.

'Maybe the clones are used for something else, too,' Edwin carried on. 'We just don't know what.'

Janus began to pace up and down. 'We need to think very carefully about this. There seems to be no immediate threat of danger, so we have time.'

Mersium nodded, but he looked troubled. 'I have been wondering why the final clone was in the cave alone. Why did he survive?'

'And why didn't he leave – try to get away?' Edwin added.

'I think that's quite obvious, Edwin,' Perpetua said sniffily. 'These clones appear to be bred with little intelligence or will of their own. He probably didn't have the brains to get out of there or find his way home.'

'So how did he survive in the cave?' Edwin said. 'What did he eat?'

'Not much, I bet. I suppose over the few years he was in there he might have eaten any creature that wandered too close to the cave. But you saw how thin he was – it was probably because he was suffering from starvation that he collapsed and died.'

Everyone stared at the bones. Edwin blinked. Shadow Magic had been shown to do some terrible things in the past. What could *this* mean?

'So what are we gonna do?' said Edwin.

'For the moment, nothing,' replied Janus. 'Thanks to Perpetua we now know the remains are clones, but they have been in Hysteria for two or three years without causing any difficulties. We need to consider our actions.'

Although Edwin still felt shaken, this was the last thing he wanted to hear. He'd got through what would surely be the worst part of this adventure and he wanted to steam ahead and help Hysteria. But Perpetua took Edwin's arm and suddenly tiredness overwhelmed him. He needed to rest, needed to sleep. He just hoped today's ordeal wouldn't bring an even more vivid Umbrian clone into his dreams . . .

CHAPTER EIGHT

EDWIN SLEPT ALL AFTERNOON AND thankfully he didn't have any nightmares (unless he counted the dream about Perpetua marking his end-of-term chemistry test).

By the time he woke up, Perpetua was bouncing off the walls with boredom. After after half an hour of nagging, Edwin tagged along with her and Bellwin in hope of finding something to do.

Perpetua was still hoping Lorius would give her a few lessons in Hysterian science, so she decided they should go to his chambers. Edwin was pretty sure Lorius would say no and then they'd be able to go off and find something else to occupy them.

They were just approaching the passage that led to

Lorius's chambers when they heard voices. It was Lorius and Janus. They were speaking quietly, but the echo of the passage carried their words quite clearly.

'. . . now we have the relic here, the Protector of the Relics should be consulted.'

'Yes, Sire. And what are we to say?'

'What Edwin has told us. I—'

'What about *me*?' Perpetua blurted to Edwin, letting her pride get the better of her. She stopped dead and clamped her hand over her mouth. Edwin shook his head. All those brains and she couldn't button her lip when absolutely necessary.

Lorius came flying around the passage. His long, thin face was white with anger. 'Are you spying on us?' he demanded. 'How long have you been there?'

"Course we're not spying on you,' Edwin said as innocently as he could. He craned his neck as the king came into view. 'We were just coming to ask you something when we heard your voices.'

'We were not hiding,' Bellwin added. 'We could not help but hear, Lorius.'

Lorius opened his mouth to speak, but Janus held up a hand. 'What *did* you hear, Bellwin?'

Perpetua cleared her throat. 'That you've decided to see the Protector of the Relics.'

Edwin glanced at her. Only Janus and Lorius were allowed in the secret chamber, but he knew exactly what she was thinking.

Sure enough, Perpetua said, 'Is there any chance we can come with you . . . ?'

Edwin felt a tingle run down his spine. The secret chamber was one of the most amazing things he'd ever seen. It would be fascinating to visit it again *and* to find out who was the new Protector of the Relics.

Lorius scoffed. 'And why would we let you into the Secret Chamber?' he demanded.

'Well, it sounded as if you want to tell the protector what we know,' replied Perpetua. 'What's the point of them hearing it third hand?'

Edwin nodded. 'Chinese whispers.'

'He means if *you* tell the protector what we know, Your Majesty, some information may be lost,' added Perpetua.

Janus looked at Perpetua for a few seconds, then threaded his fingers. 'You have both been in the chamber before, so I cannot see the harm.' He turned to Lorius. 'What do you think, my lord?'

'The harm,' snapped Lorius impatiently, 'would come from their presence when the password is given.' He glanced from Edwin to Perpetua. 'They are of course friends of Hysteria, but who knows what unintentional damage they can do if they decide to visit the chamber *alone*.'

Edwin folded his arms, but he knew Lorius was right. In this place they couldn't keep themselves to themselves.

Bellwin took a step forward. 'Surely Edwin and Perpetua could go into the chamber once the current password has been said. They do not need to hear it.'

Janus nodded. 'Yes. That would solve the problem, Bellwin. The door from the gallery does not lock until the wall into the chamber disappears.'

Edwin's spine began to tingle: this was starting to look good. 'So,' he said, 'as soon as you've said the password we leg it in before the door shuts.'

Perpetua gave an enormous sigh. 'Edwin,' she muttered. 'Do speak proper English.' She looked at Janus. 'He means we get into the room as fast as we can.'

Bellwin took a deep breath. 'Can I come too?' he asked timidly.

Janus hesitated, but smiled. 'Edwin and Perpetua are coming with us, so I do not see how I can refuse you.'

Bellwin looked at Edwin and tried to smother a grin.

'I'm totally up for it,' Edwin said.

Perpetua clasped her hands together. 'When are you going, Your Majesty?'

Janus looked from Perpetua to Edwin, then dipped his hand into his pocket and took out the relic. 'This very night,' he replied.

Lorius huffed and shook his head, but Janus ignored him. 'Would you like to lead the way, Edwin?'

They arrived at the Portrait Gallery to find Eifus and

Dreifus arguing. The brothers stood staring up at a portrait of a woman, both holding a piece of paper and a quill.

Edwin stood between them and took a peek. On Eifus's piece of paper was written *Eugranny Gonk* and on Dreifus's was *Gargantua Gonk*.

Edwin raised his eyebrows. 'Is that a relative of yours?'

Eifus looked up at Edwin with an expression of wonderment. 'Goodness! You are right. What told you, young sir?'

Edwin pointed to the word *Gonk*. 'That kinda gave it away.'

'Ah. I thought it may have been the painting itself.' Dreifus gestured to the portrait. The woman was really rather attractive, with delicate features and long blonde hair.

'Hmmm. The similarity is very subtle,' Bellwin commented.

'Do you think so, Master Bellwin?' said Eifus quite frostily. 'My brother and I have often been likened to our Great, Great Aunt Eugranny.' Dreifus snorted, but Eifus carried on. 'See the gentle sweep of the nose; the brightness of the eyes; the rich complexion of the skin.'

Dreifus folded his arms. 'For pity's sake, dear brother. That is *not* Eugranny Gonk. It is our third cousin four times removed, Miss Gargantua Gonk.'

'No, no, no, no, no!' Eifus said, patting his twin on the head with each word. 'I have already told you, brother dear, that she is wearing the brooch belonging to the more *wealthy* part of the family. The only time Gargantua Gonk wore something on her dress was when she sneezed.'

Edwin looked at Bellwin. 'He's talking about bogeys,' Edwin whispered. 'We've already told you what they are.'

'Eifus . . . Dreifus,' Janus sighed. 'What are you *doing*?'

Eifus bowed to the king. 'As curators of the gallery, Your Majesty, we have hung this portrait of Eugranny Gonk and wish to have a name plate made.'

'It is Gargantua Gonk!' Dreifus snapped.

'No it is not!' Eifus spat and elbowed his brother in the head. 'But first, Sire, we need to agree who exactly the lady in question is.' He looked around. 'Do you good people have time to help us investigate?'

'No,' Janus and Lorius replied as one.

The king turned on his heel and strode away.

'I don't think that lady could have been an ancestor of Eifus and Dreifus,' Perpetua whispered as she hurried along. 'She looked far too normal.'

Everyone gathered outside the door at the end of the gallery. Edwin suddenly felt cold and rubbed his arms. At night there was little heat or light up here. He stared at the door's unremarkable wooden panels. Who would think that on the other side was something so extraordinary?

'Edwin, wait here with Perpetua and Bellwin,' Janus

said. 'I will give the password and Lorius will wait by the door and tell you when to enter.'

The king opened the door and he and Lorius slipped through. Edwin, Perpetua and Bellwin sidled close together and waited.

'We three are indeed very privileged,' Bellwin said. 'There are many who would relish the chance to enter the Secret Chamber. How I have been permitted to enter a second time I shall never know.'

The door swung open and Lorius threw back his arm. 'Enter!' he instructed.

Edwin, Perpetua and Bellwin scuttled through, looking up just in time to see the last few of the wall's bricks disappear. Janus stood at the stop of stone steps, silhouetted by soft light. Behind him Edwin could see the quivering image of the secret chamber.

'Follow me,' the king said, stepping through the hole. Once in the room, his outline jumped as if he were in an old black-and-white film. Lorius went next, then turned to wait for Edwin and Perpetua. Edwin ran up the steps and peered over the threshold. He could see through the floor of the chamber down to the cobbles surrounding the castle, hundreds of metres below. He had to close his eyes for a second and steady himself. It still felt weird. He opened his eyes a fraction, took a step into the light and then yelped as his foot hit firm ground.

Perpetua followed and then Bellwin came in last.

They all looked around. The ante-room of the chamber hadn't changed at all, with very little furniture and nothing on the walls.

'What is the new Protector called?' Perpetua asked.

'She is called Tivoli,' Janus replied.

'Oh, another woman!' said Perpetua. 'It's go good to see a female hold down an important role here! There seem to be so few.'

'All protectors of the relics have been female,' Janus said. 'As you know, in return for their services protectors are not subject to the forces of time for many hundreds of years. We found that mainly women were tempted by the chance to retain their youth for so long.'

Perpetua stuck her nose in the air. 'You know that is what we call sexist, Your Majesty?' She looked to Edwin for support.

He raised his eyebrows and thought of the fog of hairspray outside the girls toilets – and the fact that the boys barely even bothered with deodorant. Edwin shrugged. 'Do you really want to get into a battle of the sexes right now?'

'I would not *let* you get into a battle now,' Lorius spat. 'It seems we are all going to see the protector and we should not delay.'

Janus led the way to an open door and passed through. For some reason Edwin expected the new Protector of the Relics to look and behave just like the old one, Saleena. But she couldn't have been more different. Where it had seemed as if Saleena spent most of her time gazing into a hand mirror, Tivoli didn't seem to worry what she looked like. She wore the same kind of white toga, but it was crumpled and far too big. Her hair was left long, without any decoration, and she was hunched over a book with two more sat beside her.

'Hello,' Tivoli said, taking a few seconds to look up. 'Your Majesty, it is nice to see you again so soon.' She smiled as she noticed Lorius and the others. 'Why,' she added. 'I do not think I have ever had so many visitors to the chamber!'

'Hello, good lady Tivoli,' said Janus, taking her hand. 'These young people have been in the secret chamber before.' He glanced at Bellwin. 'Without my permission, unfortunately. But there is no harm in them accompanying Lorius and me. They are Bellwin, Edwin and Perpetua.'

Tivoli stood up and looked at Bellwin. 'You must have spoken with Saleena,' she said. 'Sadly, I did not ever meet her. But I have been told how courageously she protected the relics.'

Perpetua peered at the book in Saleena's hand. 'What's that you're reading?'

'It is a study of all wars fought in these territories – by my very favourite author, Minimianna Garuder. I love her writing . . . It shows us where we have come from and who we are.'

Perpetua looked at the cover. 'Goodness, you people

do have some complicated names. And it'd be impossible to forget *that* one!' She smiled. 'Is this what you do with all of your time here – read?'

Tivoli nodded. 'Yes . . . what else would I do? Apart from watch over the relics, of course.'

'All Saleena did was stare at her reflection,' Edwin said flatly.

'Yes, I know she did not study. But I understand she was a woman who took great pride in her exceptional beauty.'

'I think you've got the right idea,' Perpetua said. 'If I was here I'd read anything I could get my hands on.' She glanced at the other books, then knelt down. 'Is that *Ancient Relics of These Territories*? We were looking for that in the library.'

'Yes, I have been reading it.' Saleena looked at Janus. 'I have sensed that what was lost has returned to Hysteria, Sire,' she added cryptically. 'Has it been found at last?'

'Edwin and Perpetua are aware of what has happened,' Janus said gently. 'That is why we are all here. The relic in question *has* been found. It was with them.'

'Saleena's eyes widened. 'Was it one of you that touched the relic?'

'We both did,' Edwin replied. 'I didn't even find out it was in my house until last week. It'd been there since I was born.'

Saleena eyes widened. 'How strange,' she whispered.

'Do you have the relic now?'

'It is here,' Janus replied, opening his hand.

Tivoli almost dived on the pendant. She studied it for a few moments, then scrambled to the floor to pick up *Ancient Relics of These Territories*. 'I have seen this . . . I recognise the drawing.' She flicked through several pages. 'Yes! It is exactly the same. Look, Sire.'

Janus peered down, then nodded.

'Can I see? Can I see?' Perpetua squealed. She took the book, then did a little hop. 'This is the one! Now, let's see –'

'Perpetua!' Edwin warned. 'You're kind of taking over.'

'Oh, I'm sorry!' Perpetua thrust the book back to Tivoli. '*You* read it, please, go ahead!'

Tivoli nodded then sat on the floor. So did everyone else.

'"The Sceptre of Jozeponi,"' Tivoli began. '"A small silver metallic pendant. Made in Jozeponi. Properties unknown".'

Perpetua huffed. 'Ugh! That phrase. D'you remember it, Edwin?'

'"Course I do,' Edwin replied. 'It told us a great big nothing then and it tells us a great big nothing now.'

'But we now know it is from Jozeponi,' Janus said firmly. 'Of that we were not aware.'

'Tivoli, is there anything else from this book that may help us?' Lorius asked.

Tivoli frowned, then shook her head. 'I can think of nothing.'

'So,' Perpetua said. 'When you sensed that the relic was being handled, was that the first you knew of it? There was nothing before that?'

'No, nothing,' Tivoli replied. 'I was appointed as protector less than a year ago, but in that time had not sensed any movement of the sceptre until a few days ago.'

'Do you know if Saleena sensed anything when she was here?' Edwin asked.

'I am afraid I do not.'

'The relic seems to have been a connection between the queen and a spirit guide,' Janus said. 'Were you aware of that?'

'No, Sire.'

'It could of course have more than one purpose,' Perpetua said. 'I don't suppose you have any idea . . .?'

Tivoli sighed. 'These relics have been amongst us for thousands of years and for some their purposes have been forgotten.'

'Of course the person who made the relic would know,' Lorius said smoothly. 'But they would be long dead.'

'Well, why don't we go to where it was made – Jozeponi?' said Perpetua.

No one said anything and she shrugged. 'It's only an idea.'

'You know, Perpetua, I think it is a good one,' Janus replied. 'We have come to a crossroads with the mystery of the remains and we do not know which way to turn. Perhaps it will do us good to think about the relic for a while and a few days away from Emporium Castle may help to sharpen our wits.'

Perpetua's eyes brightened. 'What d'you think, Edwin?'

He blinked. As far as he knew the Hysterians hadn't had any trouble from Jozeponi. It was where Janus's wife had come from, after all.

'I don't see why not,' Edwin said. He felt Lorius staring at him, but chose to ignore it.

'Then we will go,' Janus announced, before adding with a sigh, 'There is someone in Jozeponi who I have not seen in many years and I should put that right.'

'Who is it, Your Majesty?' Edwin asked without even thinking.

'The Queen's cousin – Georgiara,' Janus replied quietly.

'Don't you get on with her?' said Perpetua.

Janus looked up. 'No, my dear. That is not the case.' He rubbed his forehead then took a breath. 'Ahven was very active when she was carrying Auvlin and I told her she should rest in the month before the birth was due. She did not listen and two weeks before her time she travelled to the home of Georgiara's parents in Jozeponi. The labour started soon after she arrived and Auvlin was born there.'

Edwin raised his eyebrows. 'Ollwin told us that the queen wasn't here when she gave birth to Auvlin, but I didn't realise she wasn't even in Hysteria.'

Janus nodded. 'Away from Emporium Castle she was not under the care of my physicians.'

Perpetua bit her lip. 'If she had been,' she said carefully, 'would she have lived?'

'I do not know, Perpetua. I urged Ahven to take a court physician with her, but she insisted that her time was not imminent. She said she had been told so by a spirit guide.' He shook his head. 'I have never been comfortable with such matters, but Ahven's trust in the spirit world was life-long. And she said that her cousin's company would bring her great comfort.'

'They were fond of one another?' Bellwin asked.

'Oh, yes. They shared many interests – painting, spiritualism, the intertwined histories of Hysteria and Jozeponi. Ahven's family has had close links with the Janus line for centuries,' the king added before returning to his story. 'When I was told Ahven had gone into labour, I travelled to Jozeponi to be by her side. I did not arrive for the birth of Auvlin, but by the time I did the queen was already ill.'

'And the doctors there couldn't help her?' Edwin said.

'The doctors who had been at Auvlin's birth had been sent away by Ahven herself,' Janus replied. 'I asked

Ahven why, but what she told me was not clear. Had she let them stay, perhaps she would not have contracted a fever.'

Perpetua frowned. 'So as soon as Auvlin was born the queen told the doctors to go? That doesn't sound like the right thing to do.'

'I agree, Perpetua, but Ahven was a stubborn woman. She would not even tell me who the doctors were so I could not summon them back to the house. We had to send for my own.' Janus looked down. 'It was too late. They could not save her.'

Edwin swallowed. Why would the queen do that? What was she scared of?

'Georgiara took Ahven's death very badly and in the years since I could not find the strength to return to Jozeponi. But she may know something about how Ahven came to possess the sceptre, which may help us.'

Lorius cleared his throat. 'I am not convinced that is the best course of action, Sire. But I know how much the mystery of the relic puzzles you.'

Janus stared at the floor and everyone sat quietly for a few minutes. Tivoli was the one to break the silence.

'What you find in Jozeponi may bring you some comfort, Your Majesty,' she said. 'It is always best to reveal the truth.'

Janus looked up. There were tears in his eyes. 'Thank you, Tivoli.' He got to his feet. 'I have made up my mind – we will go to Jozeponi tomorrow.'

Edwin reached out for the king's arm. 'Us too?' he said.

Janus clasped Edwin's hand. 'Of course. I would not consider it without you.' Janus smiled and Edwin's stomach did a back flip.

'I am obliged, Tivoli,' said the king. 'There is nothing to report on the other relics?'

'No, Your Majesty. All is well.'

Everyone shook Tivoli's hand and Perpetua hung back slightly. 'Enjoy your reading,' she said, adding, 'In some ways, I envy you,' before she followed Janus.

Edwin glanced back before he went through the door. He could think of nothing worse to do with near-eternity.

CHAPTER NINE

THEY'D BEEN TRAVELLING SINCE THE previous morning and, considering what he'd been through since he'd left Earth, Edwin didn't feel too bad. He'd had a few more clone-related nightmares, but Bellwin had given him a potion to calm him down and now he felt ready for anything. And it felt like Hysteria did something to him – it seemed to make him stronger.

Edwin had spent most of the journey riding alongside Janus and Auvlin, while Perpetua had spent every waking second teaching Bellwin and Delius what she knew about the human body. 'That boy is a genius,' she'd whispered to Edwin at one point. Perpetua didn't say which boy and Edwin didn't need to ask.

The journey through Jozeponi had taken them through several villages and Edwin was glad to find that the people here looked as friendly as they did in Hysteria. When they passed through an open-air market Edwin looked around him at the sweet stalls, fruit and vegetables for sale, kittens looking for a home, and realised that in some ways this world was very similar to his own.

The sun was fairly low in the sky as the King's Guard lead the procession up a slope. Janus looked from Auvlin to Edwin. 'We are only a few minutes away from the house of Georgiara's family. They are not expecting us, so do not anticipate a welcome fit for royalty.' He smiled. 'To be truthful, if is often better to have little fuss.'

The ground levelled out and Edwin caught his first sight of the house. Even from a distance it looked pretty impressive. A sand-coloured mansion with two large wings, it nestled at one end of a valley with a river running right past the front.

'That looks really quite posh,' Perpetua whispered to Edwin.

The horses began to walk across the fields towards the valley. As they got closer, Edwin thought he might be able to spot a few people milling around. But there was no one. The house came into clearer view and he noticed that one of its large wooden doors had a huge hole in the middle. Closer still and he could see that several windows were broken, the walls were cracked and dirty, and at the top of the house a blue and white flag hung limp and torn.

Edwin looked at Janus. The king looked mystified.

'Was it like this before, Your Majesty?' Edwin asked.

'No,' Janus replied. 'It was not.' He kicked his horse into a trot, overtaking the line of soldiers in front.

'He looks a bit worried,' Edwin said to Perpetua. 'I wonder what's going on . . . '

By the time Edwin and Perpetua dismounted at the gate, Janus was peering through a broken ground floor window. 'What happened to this place?' he muttered.

Edwin joined the king and looked into what appeared to be the hallway of the house. From what he could see, it was as ill-kempt as the outside. Janus turned on his heel and summoned two soldiers.

'We will climb in through the hole in the door and attempt to open it from the inside,' he instructed.

The King climbed through first followed by the soldiers. There was the sound of grating metal, a few *tap taps* and the large doors suddenly swung back.

'Bring everyone in, Primus,' Janus said, and the King's Guard trotted through.

The courtyard was littered with junk. A broken barrel sat next to a pile of smashed plates, a wooden chair was peeling and battered from being left out in the elements and the cobbles were strewn with rubbish.

'Are you sure someone lives here?' said Perpetua. 'It

looks abandoned to me.'

'We will investigate,' Janus replied firmly and he strode towards the main door to the house.

'I bet you any money you like that it's not locked,' Edwin said to Perpetua.

'I wouldn't take that bet,' she replied. 'Because I think you're right.'

Janus pushed the door and, sure enough, it opened. One of Primus's men held it and everyone filed through. The first thing that hit Edwin was the smell. It was damp and musty, just like his gran's spare bedroom after her roof leaked. And it was so dark. Most of the windows were shuttered, with only one at the top of the staircase letting any light through, and all the surfaces were covered in dust. Every now and again the silence was broken by the sound of fluttering wings.

They stood, not speaking, until Janus stepped forward and shouted. 'Hello?'

Edwin held his breath for what seemed like ages. There was no reply.

'Hello?' Janus repeated. 'Is there anyone living here?'

Again there was nothing. Primus walked to the bottom of the staircase and looked up. 'Should we search the house, Sire?'

'Yes,' Janus murmured. 'I think we shall have to.'

Primus split his men to search the east and west wings of the first and second floor. He led one of the four groups up the stairs, while Janus, Edwin, Perpetua and Auvlin took another along the passage of the ground floor. The corridor was dark and the floor creaked with every step. The doors along the way hung open, but none seemed to lead to any sign of life. As they passed through what looked like a storage area, Edwin looked around and noticed a light.

'Look!' he whispered, pointing left.

Janus stopped dead, then walked slowly towards the door. Edwin followed and as he crept closer, he could see it was a kitchen. There was a large, bare table in the middle, but the rest of the room was as untidy as the rest of the house. Old dried-up food littered the floor and dirty cooking utensils were piled on every work surface. A solitary lamp flickered above a stone fireplace and beneath it, bent over a cooking pot, was a woman. Her slow movements gave Edwin the impression that she was fairly old, stirring the pot carefully with the air of someone who had lost the pace of youth. There were three wide, high-backed chairs facing the fireplace and over two of them Edwin could see the tops of people's heads. Whoever they were, they must be very tall.

Janus frowned and stepped forward. 'Good day, my lady.'

The woman stopped what she was doing, turned, and Edwin's eyes widened. Her hair was long and tangled, her face thin and gaunt and she had no colour apart from the dark circles around her eyes. Her dress must once have been grand; now it was old and stained.

The woman had the look of one who had faced great suffering, but at the same time Edwin could see that she was probably still only in her thirties. She put down her spoon on the table and looked straight at Janus.

'Have you come with the flour, sir?' she asked.

'Flour?' Janus repeated.

'Yes. It is our weekly order. I will be glad to receive it . . . we are running so low.' The woman picked up a jar and as she removed the top there was the sound of an empty echo. 'Please put some in here – the rest is for the store room.'

Edwin heard Janus take a stilted breath. 'Georgiara?' he murmured.

The woman frowned, but her expression showed no sign that she recognised Janus. 'I have not been called Georgiara in many, many years,' she said softly. She turned and addressed one of the chairs. 'You only called me by my full name when I was small, Father. Do you remember?' She stood still for a moment, then smiled. 'I know you are hungry, Father. There is not long to wait . . . the soup is nearly ready.'

Janus glanced at Auvlin. 'Did you hear anyone speak?'

The prince shook his head.

Janus began to walk around the wooden table. Both Edwin and Auvlin followed. They reached the end of the table and together their pace slowed.

The first two chairs did indeed have people in them; or leaning against them. A man and woman were both rigidly straight, their heels on the floor and their heads resting against the chair backs with no other part of them touching anything. Edwin frowned. What were they doing? But then more details struck him. The bodies' arms were held tight against their sides, as if they had been wedged in. Their faces were expressionless, eyes staring straight ahead and mouths slewed into an unnatural line. He moved closer and saw that their skin was thickened and yellow. Edwin stumbled to a halt. He glanced at Perpetua, trying to make sense of what he could see.

These people were dead.

Edwin's stomach churned. Saliva flooded his mouth and he fought to swallow it, wiping a wet streak from his lips. Slowly he turned to look at the third chair. Something was sitting there, but it wasn't a body. It was a padded-out dress, like the stuffed clothes of a scarecrow. A white cushion sat on top, on which had been drawn a face. It was a crude, childish drawing like that of a five-year old.

Georgiara turned back to the fireplace and ladled some soup into a bowl. She lifted the bowl towards the cushion, then took out a spoon and held it to the drawn-on lips. 'You first, dear cousin,' she said softly. 'I have made sure it is not too hot.'

Auvlin had stopped, but Janus had only hesitated for a few seconds before carrying on. Edwin wanted to tug him back. This woman was mad. She was talking to corpses and a giant doll. She might have killed these people. She *might* try to kill Janus . . .

Edwin sprang forward and grabbed Janus's hand. But the king simply gripped Edwin tight and kept shuffling forward. He looked transfixed.

Edwin's heart thumped in his throat. He didn't want to get any closer. He didn't want to see any more of these slurred, frozen faces. But Janus pulled him a few more feet, then stopped. He let go of Edwin's hand and Edwin edged into the king's back.

'Georgiara,' Janus whispered. 'What is it you are doing?'

'I am giving my dear parents and cousin their lunch.' Georgiara put a full spoon to the lips of the dead man's body and smiled. 'They are always so tired . . . I like to look after them.' She put down the bowl, picked up a napkin and dabbed the man's lips. 'There, Father. Have you had enough?'

Janus turned back to Edwin and Auvlin. 'I do not think she will hurt us . . .'

But Edwin didn't want to venture much further forward. He craned his neck and looked again at the dead man. Somehow he didn't look real . . . like a badly-made wax model. The whites of his eyes had turned a dull grey and the hand that was visible was mottled, the fingers slightly clawed. There was a smell, not of rotting flesh, but a strong, cloying smell that made Edwin think of death. He felt his stomach churn for a second time, and again he looked at Perpetua.

'They're dead,' he mouthed.

Janus reached out. 'Georgiara,' he said gently. 'Can you take my hand?'

Georgiara looked at Janus's hand, then at his face. 'Who are you, sir?'

'I am . . . a friend,' Janus replied.

Georgiara stared for a few seconds, then put her hand in the king's. 'Why, your skin is so warm, sir,' she said quickly. 'Are you in poor health?'

Janus glanced at Edwin, sorrow welling in his eyes. 'I am quite well, thank you. Come and sit at the table with me.'

While Janus and Georgiara took their seats, everyone else came to stand around them. Edwin edged his way over to Bellwin and Perpetua.

'Did you say that person was dead?' Perpetua hissed in his ear.

'There's *two* dead bodies,' Edwin replied. 'And one thing that looks like a woman scarecrow. You know . . . a stuffed dress and a pillow with a face.'

Perpetua swallowed. 'What do the bodies look like?'

'They're not rotting. Their skin looks sort of thick and yellow.'

She looked at Georgiara. 'My God, the poor thing. What's happened to them? What's happened to *her*?'

The whispers between the group fell quiet and everyone looked at Georgiara.

'How long have you been on your own here?' Janus asked softly.

Georgiara blinked. 'But I am not on my own, sir. I have my mother and father and cousin. I have lived here all my life. The servants have gone and only we four remain.'

'And your father and mother and cousin are always seated in this room?'

'Yes, sir. They spend all their time there as it is very comfortable. I do not like to move them to another part of the house when they are so happy here.'

Janus paused, then took a deep breath. 'What is the name of your cousin, my dear?'

Georgiara smiled. 'She is called Ahven, sir.'

Edwin saw the king's bottom lip tremble. Auvlin moved to stand behind Janus and put his hand on his shoulder.

'That is a beautiful name,' the king croaked. He took a moment to recover. 'Has she lived with your family for long?'

'She came to this house many, many years ago . . . when I was not yet twenty. I brought her here. She has been my constant companion.'

Janus glanced up at his son. 'And did she bring anyone with her?'

Georgiara frowned, then shook her head. 'No, sir. A few days after we arrived she became very ill, as I remember.'

'You say she was ill?' Janus said carefully. 'Did she make a full recovery?'

'Why yes, sir. You only have to look at Ahven. She looks quite well!'

Janus didn't look over to the chairs, but he smiled softly. 'Yes, of course,' he said. 'Tell me, does the name Janus mean anything to you?'

Georgiara thought for a few moments, then replied, 'Do you mean the king of Hysteria?' She kept looking at Janus, but her expression didn't change; her memory didn't seem to be stirred.

Janus sighed and looked down at the table, then reached out and patted Georgiara's hand. 'You need to tend to your family,' he said gently. 'Do not let me delay you.'

The king got slowly to his feet. His face had drained of all colour. He walked slowly from the room and beckoned everyone to follow.

Janus needed some air. He led everyone out to the courtyard and leaned against a wall to steady himself. 'Poor, unfortunate woman,' he muttered, putting his hand to his forehead. 'She is living in a world of dreams and delusions.' He waived his hand. 'Please leave me alone for a moment.'

Auvlin put his hand on his father's shoulder, then led Edwin, Perpetua and Bellwin away to talk.

'Has Georgiara forgotten what happened to Queen Ahven?' Edwin said in hushed tones. 'She doesn't even know who the king is, or that he was married to her.'

'Or that I was born here,' Auvlin added.

Perpetua threaded her fingers. 'She seems to have blocked the whole thing out. It's a known medical condition on Earth – a way of coping with a terrible event.'

'Forgetting stuff is one thing,' Edwin whispered. 'But thinking a stuffed dress is an actual person is something else.'

'And the bodies,' Bellwin added weakly. 'It is obvious she thinks that her parents are still alive.' He looked around. 'They *are* dead, are they not?'

'No doubt about that,' Perpetua replied firmly. 'From what Edwin told me, I think they've been preserved somehow.'

They all stood in silence for a few moments. Then Auvlin spoke.

'I am afraid that if Georgiara is not of sound mind then she may remember nothing about my mother's relic. After all, she has forgotten about the pregnancy, about me being born and that my mother and father were married.'

Edwin shook his head. 'But she seems to remember *some* things, like her bringing Ahven here and that soon after Ahven was ill.'

'I think Edwin's right,' said Perpetua. 'Georgiara's

memories seem patchy, but not completely absent. So,' she added, looking around. 'Has anyone got any idea what we should do next?'

'If I know my father,' Auvlin replied. 'He will want to make sure Georgiara is strong enough to cope with our presence. He will want to tend to her and nourish her. And surely we should do something about *this*,' he added, gesturing around. 'We should put her home in good order.'

'Should we bury the bodies?' said Edwin.

'I do not know,' Auvlin murmured. 'Perhaps forcing Georgiara's to realise that her parents are dead may be too much for her to bear.'

'I wonder *how long* they've been dead?' Edwin whispered.

'Surely there would be some sort of record somewhere,' said Perpetua.

'You know what I think,' Edwin carried on. 'Those bodies have already been put in some sort of coffin, then after a while taken out again. It's their arms . . . straight by their sides like they've been lying in a narrow space or something.'

'Ugghh . . . of course,' Perpetua said weakly. 'They've been exhumed. That's just horrible!'

'They do not burn the bodies in Jozeponi, as we do in Hysteria,' Auvlin cut in. 'I believe that most are kept in underground rooms, with each family together.'

'Some of our civilisations used to do that,' Perpetua

said. 'The rooms are known as crypts.'

The hairs on the back of Edwin's neck stood up. 'Auvlin,' he said weakly, 'where d'you reckon these rooms would be in *this* kingdom?'

When the prince looked at him, Edwin knew what was coming next. 'In the family houses. It may well be beneath where we were standing.'

Edwin and Perpetua exchanged a look. They each knew what the other was thinking – one way or another, they were going to end up down there.

CHAPTER TEN

THE FOLLOWING MORNING JANUS PERSUADED Georgiara that her 'mother and father' didn't look comfortable in the kitchen, and he had their bodies placed side by side in their bedroom. At first Georgiara had wanted to stay with them, but Perpetua convinced her they needed proper rest and should not be disturbed. Eventually she was happy to go up to their room to look at them every now and then. The stuffed doll remained in the kitchen, sitting by the fire.

That evening, Janus sat down with Georgiara and the others to talk. He had told her his name was Janus, but that it was just a coincidence that he had the same name as the king of Hysteria.

'How are you, Georgiara?' he began.

She smiled. The colour of her cheeks was brighter and Perpetua had put her hair into tidy plaits. Edwin thought she looked quite pretty now.

'I feel slightly different to how I did, Janus,' Georgiara replied. 'Better, I think.'

'And you are enjoying being looked after?'

'I am not used to it,' said Georgiara, blushing. 'Although it has been very nice.'

'I think you've been working too hard,' said Perpetua, squeezing her hand. 'You need to take some time to rest.'

The king nodded, then crossed his hands on his lap. 'May we ask you some questions about your life here?'

'Of course,' Georgiara replied. 'What would you like to know?' She shook her head. 'Although there is so much I cannot remember . . .'

'We will not press you,' Janus assured her. 'Can I ask about your cousin Ahven?'

'Yes! I love to talk about my cousin. Perhaps when she wakes up you could ask her some questions yourself. She is very talkative, sir.'

Janus half-smiled. 'Yes, of course,' he said. 'Tell me, did you know Ahven very well before she came to live at this house?'

'Our mothers were sisters, Janus. They both married quite young, but they still spent a lot of time with one another. When I was born, Ahven was already a

136

young woman and during my first years she was almost like a second mother to me. As I grew older our relationship changed – I regarded her as my sister and my friend.'

'So how much older than you was she?' Perpetua asked.

'Fourteen years,' Georgiara replied. 'She was her mother's first child. I was an only child and my mother was considered quite old when I was born.'

'And what is your first memory of her?' Janus asked.

'Taking me for a walk here, in the gardens.' Georgiara looked up at a window. 'I remember her hand being very soft. She walked slowly so that I did not have to hurry.' She looked back at Janus. 'I remember her face smiling down at me.'

Janus swallowed. Edwin sensed that he wouldn't be able to talk for a moment.

'She sounds lovely,' he eventually managed with a croak.

'Yes, she is,' Georgiara replied. 'We often remember the times when I was very young. She would have loved children of her own, but it seems it was never to be.'

Edwin glanced at Auvlin. His eyes were cast down, but it was still possible to see him blink away tears. Janus reached over and squeezed his son's hand. 'Do you remember much about how she dressed or what jewellery she wore?' he said.

'A little,' Georgiara replied. 'Her clothes were pretty,

but quite plain. She did not like to wear anything too ornate.'

Janus smiled and Edwin thought that what Georgiara had said must have rung true.

'She wore a ring that her mother had given her, but very little other jewellery.'

'So her mother's ring was a keepsake?' Perpetua asked.

'Yes, it was.'

'And was that the only keepsake she carried?'

Georgiara put her hands on her lap and seemed to look into the middle distance. 'There was also small pendant,' she said eventually. 'But she did not wear it as jewellery – she usually kept it in a purse. I feel as if I should know why, but for some reason I do not.'

Janus shifted in his chair. He obviously wanted to press Georgiara on this, but at the same time was looking at her with concern. 'That is not important,' he said gently. 'But do you know where the pendant came from?'

Georgiara looked at the king. 'Yes,' she said brightly. 'It came from our grandmother, Leana. My grandmother died when I was twelve, so Ahven must have been given the relic when she was a young woman.' She paused. 'Can I ask why you are so interested in my cousin, sir?'

Janus blinked, as if the bluntness of the question had taken him by surprise. 'It was her name,' he said carefully. 'I knew a woman called Ahven, and I wondered if it was by chance the same person.'

'Oh!' Georgiara said brightly. 'You did not recognise her when we first met?'

Janus shook his head. 'No.'

'But do you *think* it is the same woman?'

Janus stared at the ground. Edwin knew the king was thinking he should take the truth very slowly.

'No,' Janus repeated, barely looking up.

Edwin swallowed hard. It was at times like this that he wanted to get up and hug Janus tighter than he'd ever hugged anyone.

'What sort of things did you do together when you were older?' Perpetua asked.

'We were both interested in the spirit world,' Georgiara replied. 'We both sought guidance from mediums about the future. Ahven was once told who she would marry. She did not tell me who, but she said she would act on the advice.'

Edwin raised his eyebrows. Perpetua had been right. That *was* why she and Janus had married so quickly – she'd been told he'd ask her. She already knew they would be happy.

The wheels in Perpetua's head had obviously started turning, because she started asking more questions. 'Is there anything about Leana written down? Did she keep any records?'

'Yes, there are some . . . somewhere,' Georgiara replied vaguely. She stifled a yawn. 'But I would not know where to begin to look for them.'

Perpetua opened her mouth to say something else, but Janus stood up and offered Georgiara his hand. 'You are tired, my dear,' he said softly. 'You must rest. Let me help you to your feet.'

'Thank you, sir,' Georgiara said, taking the king's hand. 'I will go to bed now, I think.' She turned to go then hesitated. 'But I will call in on my mother and father before I retire . . . just to make sure that they are comfortable. Goodnight, everyone.'

All who were gathered mumbled *goodnight* back, and as soon as Georgiara had left the room they huddled around again to talk.

'I do not want to press the poor woman about the pendant,' Janus began. 'But she has at least given us some useful information.'

'Can I ask you, Father,' Auvlin said. 'Did you ever meet Leana?'

'Yes,' the king replied. 'Once or twice. A welcoming but rather strange lady.'

'How do you mean?' Edwin asked.

Janus frowned. 'She was active in the spirit world . . . I am sure that is why Ahven became interested in it.' He shook his head. 'I have never felt comfortable with those matters. It is not fit for a good family to dabble in such things.'

Edwin looked at Perpetua. She was itching to say something.

'Why don't we try to find out more about Leana?' she said eagerly. 'She's the person who gave the relic to Ahven, so it makes sense to start there.'

'I know where you can look,' Primus said. 'Today three of my men found hoards of papers in one of the uppermost rooms.'

'Did they?' Perpetua gasped. 'We should look through them straight away!'

Everyone nodded, except Edwin, whose eyes were on the king. Was he OK with them sticking their noses into the business of his wife's family?

'How d'you feel about it, Your Majesty?' he said gently.

Janus looked up. He smiled, but there was still sadness in his eyes. 'We do what we have to, dear Edwin. Another new day brings a new mystery.' He got slowly to his feet. 'And as with all of them, we must try to solve it.'

During breakfast the following morning it was clear to see that Perpetua was gagging to get started.

'I'm so glad Janus convinced Georgiara to put those bodies somewhere else,' she said to Edwin quietly. 'I don't think I'd have been able to stomach toast with them sitting in the room and we're going to need all the energy we can get today. Concentration uses up more of it than you might think.'

Edwin looked at her. 'You know, your brain works in a really strange way.'

Perpetua raised her eyebrows. 'It's called an enquiring mind,' she snapped. 'You'd do much better if you had one.'

'If it would make me talk like *you* do, you can keep it.' Edwin frowned. 'I wonder how much paper there is to look through . . .'

'From what Primus said last night, there's a lot.'

'So who exactly is going to sort through it?'

'You, me and Auvlin,' Perpetua said. 'Janus wants to spend some time with Georgiara without firing questions at her. He feels a bit guilty about last night.'

Edwin half-smiled. That was just like the king. 'What about everyone else?'

'They're still busy sorting the house out. Bellwin is going to try to do some of it with magic. He's taking Delius along so he can observe.' Perpetua swallowed a slug of milk then slammed her cup down on the table. 'Shall we go? You know what they say – he who hesitates is lost.'

Edwin had never actually heard anyone say that, but he thought he knew what Perpetua meant. They went to find Auvlin, then they all made their way to the room where Primus's men had found the stack of papers. He'd said there were a lot and as the three entered the room they weren't disappointed.

Four big and very dusty boxes sat in the middle of

the floor, brimming with folded letters, scripts and large rolled-up pieces of parchment. Perpetua plunged her hand into one box, then did four enormous sneezes on the trot. 'Oh by goodness,' she said snottily. 'Dese aben't been dutched in years.'

Auvlin opened a window, letting the swirl of dust out, and they got to work. Edwin decided there was actually even more paper in here than it first appeared and he started to stifle a succession of yawns. After a few hours the most interesting thing any of them had found was a drawing of Queen Ahven's wedding dress.

'That is beautiful,' Auvlin whispered when Perpetua showed it to him. 'I have always wondered what my mother looked like on her wedding day. Do you think I could take the sketch back to Emporium Castle?'

''Course,' said Edwin. 'It should belong to you and the king.'

'In our world,' said Perpetua, 'we have these machines called cameras that make things called photographs. I take a photograph of a castle, for example, and the image appears on paper just as I had seen it earlier.'

Auvlin looked fascinated. 'How incredible. And what else do you take 'photographs' of? '

'We take photographs of anything and everything,' Edwin replied. 'A few weeks ago me and my friend Nat went to a photo booth – that's like a box that takes photos of people for a laugh – and we got some prints of us pulling some really stupid faces and me sticking my fingers up my nose!'

Edwin giggled – he thought it was hilarious. Auvlin just looked a bit puzzled. 'Edwin!' Perpetua snapped. 'That is totally crass and very, very immature.'

'Yeah, I know. It was brilliant!'

Towards the end of the afternoon Edwin's work rate was slowing, but Perpetua was still going great guns. 'Oh, look at this,' she yelped suddenly. 'I've found Ahven and Georgiara's family tree. It was tied in a bundle with all these other papers, so they might say something about Leana.'

Perpetua split the bundle into three and gave each of them a pile to look through. It was only a few minutes before Auvlin sat up, waving a handful of pages in the air.

'Here is some information,' he yelped. 'Come and sit by me. I shall read it to you.'

Edwin and Perpetua sat either side of the prince.

'They look like notes,' Perpetua said. 'The writing is quite childish . . .'

'It is not my mother's,' said Auvlin.

'But look!' Perpetua said, jabbing the paper with her finger. 'A few lines down – "This record is taken from a conversation with my grandmother." Last night Georgiara said her grandmother died when she was twelve.'

'Exactly,' said Edwin, trying to sound as if he'd worked that out before Perpetua had. 'Maybe it was a sort of project – like what we do at school with family trees and that.'

Auvlin looked from one to the other, then took a deep breath and started to read. '"Leana was born during the time of a war between Jozeponi and Umbria. Her mother, father and their family went to the mountains to avoid the fighting, and Leana was born there. They had been in the mountains for many weeks and no one was sure of the exact date of her birth. When she was eighteen, my grandmother was able to discover it by other means.'

Auvlin stopped reading, and Perpetua said, 'Other means? Does it say what they were?'

Auvlin scanned down the page. 'I cannot see anything . . . ' he said.

'I think I can guess,' said Perpetua. 'The spirit world – Georgiara and Ahven made use of it, and I bet their grandmother did too.'

Everyone nodded, and Perpetua added, 'Carry on, Auvlin.'

Auvlin read another page, which talked about Leana's childhood. As he flipped over to the next his pace began to slow. '". . . her interest in magic and the spiritualism began . . . as a young woman . . . "' Auvlin glanced up at Perpetua.

'What did I tell you,' she said. '*That's* how she found

out her date of birth. If no one knew the date for sure when she was born, they're not going to know it years and years later. She found out with some sort of medium or magic – mark my words.' She reached over. 'So does it go into any detail?' said Perpetua, gently tugging the paper from Auvlin's hands.

He gave it up without a fight. Perpetua concentrated for a few minutes, her lips moving silently as she read to herself. Then she said, 'Leana took guidance in prophecy from Pepsil the Second, a spiritualist who lived on the northern border of Jozeponi. He taught her some of his skills and gave her many tools of prophecy, including runic stones, an ancient relic and a ring.' Perpetua's eyes widened. 'Is that *our* relic?'

Edwin nodded. 'If I had to put money on it then I'd say yes.'

Perpetua sighed and looked at Auvlin. 'He means if he had to make a bet,' she said, hoping that was a word in Hysteria. But Auvlin still looked blank.

'On Earth,' said Edwin, 'we have places where horses and dogs run races, and people can win money from the bookies if they predict which ones will win. We call it making bets.'

'Bookies?' Auvlin repeated. 'So these races are held in libraries?'

Edwin raised his eyebrows. 'Nah,' he said flatly. 'That's probably the last place you'd find them.'

'It doesn't really matter,' Perpetua said impatiently.

'Edwin is saying he thinks the relic Pepsil the Second gave to Leana *is* the Sceptre of Jozeponi.' She frowned. 'I just wish there was more detail. We know it was some sort of tool for prophecy, but what exactly did it do?'

'Hmmm,' Edwin agreed. 'Maybe this bloke's name will jog Georgiara's memory?'

'I don't think that's likely,' Perpetua replied. 'Although anything is worth a try.'

But when the three went to find Georgiara they were told that Janus had taken her somewhere, along with Primus and half the King's Guard.

'It seems Janus has found out something important,' Bellwin told them. 'Georgiara showed him some family records – the wedding of her older sister – and among the list of guests was the name of a physician.'

Auvlin's eyes widened. 'Her father's physician? The one who attended my mother when I was born?'

'Janus could not ask Georgiara, of course, as she has no memory of it.'

'So is that where he's gone?' asked Perpetua.

'Yes, to see if this physician is still alive and if he can shed any light on what happened that night.'

Edwin felt quite deflated. He didn't like it when Janus went anywhere without him. 'How long is he going to be?'

'Janus said he would stay away no longer than a day,' Delius replied. 'That whatever happened, he would be back tomorrow.'

'Half of the King's Guard has remained here,' Bellwin said. 'So we are still well protected.'

Edwin looked at the piece of paper in Perpetua's hand. 'Shame Georgiara isn't here. And Janus. We've got something to show them.'

Bellwin's eyes widened and he moved towards Perpetua. 'What is it?'

But at that moment a soldier appeared at the door. 'Wizard Bellwin,' he said quickly. 'We require your assistance.'

Bellwin hesitated, obviously wanting to stay where he was, but he looked at Delius. 'Come with me,' he instructed. He turned back before he reached the door. 'Can you tell me all this later?' he asked. 'I will return as soon as I can.'

'Yeah,' Edwin replied. 'But don't be too long – this is gonna burn a hole in Perpetua's pocket.'

If that had indeed been true the whole mansion would have been on fire, as the young wizards didn't return until night had fallen. Perpetua made sure enough food was kept back for Bellwin and Delius and as they both walked into the kitchen they looked dead on their feet.

'So much work,' Bellwin yawned as he sat at the table. 'If Ollwin were here he would not allow magic to be used for so many practical tasks – Hysteria's crystals are precious.'

'But we were a great help,' Delius added brightly. He looked at Edwin. 'I believe you had something interesting to show us?'

It was actually Perpetua and Auvlin who told them all about what they'd discovered. Both Bellwin and Delius looked transfixed as they ate their meal and Bellwin was the first to speak up when Perpetua had finished.

'You would think,' he said, 'that if the relic was made in Jozeponi and owned by the family here in *this* house, there would be another scrap of information somewhere. It is as if the purpose of the relic is a deadly secret.'

Perpetua sat up, cleared her throat and turned to Auvlin. She looked as if she was about to ask something controversial. 'Auvlin, I know that in Hysteria the dead are usually cremated, but do you know much about the burial traditions of other kingdoms?'

'Yes, I have some knowledge.'

'Well let me ask you this – when someone dies in Jozeponi, is it possible for items to be buried with them – you know, their possessions?'

Auvlin nodded. 'It is not an unusual practice,' he replied. 'Why do you ask? What are you thinking?'

'Well, if Bellwin is right and the purpose of the relic is secret, I wonder whether Leana was buried with something that might give us some clues.'

'Right!' Edwin blurted. But then he frowned; he'd realised exactly where this was going.

'If this house *does* have a crypt,' Perpetua continued, 'Maybe we could go down there and just have a look.'

Edwin stared at Perpetua. He'd heard the words she'd said, but his brain was having trouble processing the notion that she might actually mean them. 'You know, when Auvlin said this place might have a crypt, I had a feeling we'd end up down there. What I *didn't* think was that you'd plan on opening a few coffins.'

He looked from Perpetua to Auvlin and back again. They looked quite excited and were therefore clearly both bonkers.

'I have opened coffins before,' Auvlin replied. 'And I lived to tell the tale.'

This surprised Edwin so much it was a little while before he could speak. 'When did, er . . . when did you do that, then?' he asked eventually.

'It was not long before you first came to Hysteria. Some of the King's Guard had been killed in a small border skirmish ten years before and were buried at the scene of the battle. My father wanted to return their remains to their families and I helped his men identify which of the dead were Hysterian.'

Perpetua looked intrigued. 'How were they buried?'

'In wooden coffins. The surrounding soil must have contained a preserving element, as the process of decay had been delayed.'

'They weren't just bones, then?' Edwin asked.

'No. Flesh was still upon them.'

'Having seen Georgiara's parents,' Perpetua said, 'I think that's what we'll find in the crypt, too. If she's there, Leana will be very well preserved rather than a putrefying mess.'

Edwin grimaced. He wasn't quite sure which would be worse.

'So if we choose to go into the crypt, Edwin,' the prince said, 'I will be able to perform the practical tasks.'

Edwin wasn't sure whether that was any consolation. He didn't want to go down into a room full of dead bodies. He didn't want to see the lid being ripped off a coffin. He didn't want to watch Auvlin lift up a waxy yellow hand and tug a clue from cold, stiff fingers. But for some reason he didn't say so.

'OK. Let's do it.'

CHAPTER ELEVEN

EDWIN ASSUMED THEY WOULD TAKE the relic into the crypt, but that evening he started to wonder if it might spark some kind of terrible reaction. After all, the relic contained a spirit guide and the crypt was going to contain *loads* of dead bodies. Perpetua suggested that was all the more reason to take it since they were going down there to try to discover the relic's secret. Edwin still felt a bit jumpy, but after a short argument Perpetua put the relic in her pocket. Edwin, in turn, insisted that several soldiers accompany them.

Delius found a plan of the house and worked out quite easily where the entrance to the crypt was. But by the time they were ready to go it was very late indeed.

'I wish it was still day time,' Edwin said as he stared at a black wooden door.

'That would not make an iota of difference,' Perpetua replied. 'Light doesn't pass underground. Duh!'

Auvlin volunteered to go into the crypt first. He would take a lit torch and check that all was safe, then the others would join them. But when he came back up he shook his head.

'What's the matter?' whispered Edwin. 'Is it full of zombies?'

Auvlin looked straight at Perpetua and she said, 'That's the walking dead who come back to life.'

'Ah, I see. Well, no . . .' Auvlin replied.

'So is there, like, nothing down there at all?' Edwin continued. 'Have the bodies disappeared?' He looked around. 'Maybe Georgiara's got them stacked up all around the house.'

'No, Edwin. There are many, many coffins in the crypt. So many, in fact, that not more than four or five people at a time can stand in the room comfortably.'

Edwin blinked. He didn't care if the crypt had more room than the Albert Hall – with a pile of dead bodies in it, he'd *never* feel comfortable.

'So that means we three can go in, plus two soldiers,' Perpetua said. 'Edwin – it's not as if we're going to be outnumbered by anything that walks and talks.'

'This isn't Earth, remember?' Edwin scoffed. '*Anything* could happen.'

'Yes, all right,' Perpetua said. 'It's *unlikely*, then.'

Edwin smirked. 'Well if you're not that worried, why don't *you* go into the crypt first?'

Perpetua stared at Edwin for a good few seconds, as if she couldn't believe he'd called her bluff. She went white, then squeaked a high-pitched, 'Fine.' She walked to the open door and stood at the top of the damp stone steps. Edwin craned his neck. It looked *really* dark down there.

Auvlin didn't seem to be in on Edwin's joke, as he smiled at Perpetua encouragingly and offered her the torch. 'Do not forget – you will need this.'

Perpetua looked into the darkness again and swallowed. 'On second thoughts,' she said, 'maybe it's best if you lead us in, Auvlin. You've already been down there.'

Edwin scoffed as Perpetua scuttled back next to him. 'You're all mouth and no trousers,' he whispered. Perpetua glanced at Auvlin and opened her mouth, but Edwin added, 'Don't bother. I don't think he heard me.'

Once again Auvlin descended the steps, the torch lighting the way. As Edwin followed, he felt nerves flood his stomach. It was getting colder, but his hands felt clammy. He could hear the sound of Perpetua's stilted breathing and Edwin held *his* breath; he didn't want to take in the stale, dead air that was down there.

They came out into a large space full to bursting with too much stuff. The flames of the torch lit up row after row of closely stacked coffins. Edwin felt his throat press for air and he let out a gasp. He closed his mouth quickly, but as soon as air streamed up his nostrils he smelt the same horrible odour he'd encountered a few days before. He swallowed and tried not to think about it.

Auvlin pointed to a row of coffins. 'The names of the dead are inscribed on the end. However there is no year, so we cannot find if there is any order to them.'

Edwin looked around and spotted two coffins empty leaning against a short stretch of wall. The lids lay on the floor. He started towards them to look at the names, but then it struck him. 'Look at those,' he said, jerking his head. 'They must have belonged to Georgiara's mother and father. D'you think she got them out of the coffins *herself*?'

'She must have,' Auvlin replied. 'There is no one else here to help.'

Edwin shook his head. 'So . . . she takes her mum out of the coffin. The body is cold and as hard as nails. It doesn't talk, it doesn't walk, the blimmin' eyes don't move. She feeds it, but it doesn't eat; she talks to it, but it doesn't talk back. And she *still* doesn't realise her mum is dead. And she does exactly the same thing with her dad. It's just *weird*.' He jolted as a shiver ran through him. 'What the hell am I doing down here?'

'Right,' Perpetua said briskly, but still with a slight shake in her voice. 'Where shall we start?'

There were several suggestions, but Perpetua didn't listen to any of them. She went straight to a stack of coffins and started to read the names from the bottom. After several seconds she glanced up.

'Come on, Edwin – get on with it. I want to get out of here as much as you do!'

Both Edwin and Auvlin got to work. Edwin didn't care how funny some of the names were – he wasn't in the mood for a laugh, and he could have danced around the coffins when a few minutes later he spotted the name Leana on a tarnished metal plaque.

'Crikey,' he said with relief. 'I think I've found her.'

Edwin stepped to one side. Auvlin and the two soldiers spent a few minutes making some space around the coffin, then slid it out of its resting place. They put it on the floor and everyone stood staring down at the lid.

'Now,' Auvlin said firmly. 'The question is: should I remove the lid here?'

'I'm not being funny,' Edwin said quickly, 'but two dead bodies up there are more than enough. Can't we just have a quick look, then shut the lid and put the coffin back where we found it?'

Auvlin asked one of the soldiers to help him remove the lid from the coffin. They took knives from their belts and ran the blades slowly along the coffin's outside seal, then inserted the blades between the lid and the coffin. The strain showed on their faces as they pushed down on the knives to try and prize off the lid, but after a few minutes of struggle it seemed stuck fast.

'Prince Auvlin,' said the other soldier. 'Edwin and I should hold the coffin down. It will help you.'

'Yes, of course,' Auvlin replied, kneeling. 'Edwin, you can take my side.'

Edwin hesitated, but he knew he had to help. He got on his knees and gripped one side of the coffin with both hands. It was difficult as there were no handles, but if he used his palms they could hold it fairly steady. 'OK,' he murmured. 'I'm ready.'

Once again Auvlin and the first soldier levered their knife blades upwards. Edwin grimaced as he strained to hold the coffin down. There was a moment's rest, then the process began again. Edwin felt the lid give a little, and there was a soft *crack*. He relaxed slightly.

'Keep going,' Auvlin urged. 'I think it is starting to come away.'

Edwin held his breath and held on as tight as he could. Despite the cold of the crypt, he was starting to sweat. His shoulders began to ache, but he kept pushing down.

There was a *thwack* of splintering wood, and Edwin strengthened his grip even more. The knives were straining at the lid, everyone gasping with the effort. Edwin didn't think he could keep going much longer. He let out his breath in a painful shudder . . .

CRACK!

Just as the lid of the coffin flew up, Edwin lost his grip. The coffin jolted and a body lifted into the air. It spun to the left and Edwin saw its face. The eyes stared straight at him from sunken sockets. Edwin yelped and scuttled backwards. His head hit a coffin and a spray of dust and cobwebs sank onto his face. Then he felt a hand on his leg and he shrieked.

'Edwin,' Perpetua whispered frantically. 'It's only me . . . it's all right. It's all right.'

Edwin scraped the cobwebs from his eyes, wiped his mouth then took in a huge gasp of air. 'It is dead, right?'

'Oh, yes,' Perpetua replied weakly. 'She's as dead as dead can be.'

Auvlin pulled Edwin to his feet. 'Do you want to go upstairs while we do this, my friend?'

'Nah, 'course not.' Edwin dusted himself down. 'It can't get any worse than that, can it?' He took a step forward and peered into the coffin. The body was back in its resting place, bulging eyes now staring up at the ceiling, arms rigid as if bolted to its sides. The flesh of the face had shrunk into a tight cover of yellow skin, pulling back the lips to expose blackened gums and teeth.

Auvlin put his hands into the coffin, turned the corpse to one side and looked underneath

'Nothing here.'

He leaned over and moved the body towards him.

Edwin and Perpetua peered in, but that side of the coffin was empty too.

Auvlin laid the corpse back down. 'Is there any jewellery?' he murmured.

Sure enough, Leana's left hand was dressed with a ring. Auvlin was able to slide it off the shrunken fingers very easily, and as he held it up to the light Edwin glimpsed a pattern.

'I think we should get the pendant out,' Auvlin said hesitantly. 'It looks to be a little similar . . .'

Edwin took the box out of his pocket and opened it. 'You can get it out,' he said to Perpetua. 'I'm not gonna touch it.'

Perpetua looked at Edwin. 'Of course,' she said, just a bit too sweetly. She took the pendant out of the box and dangled it over Edwin's hand. Then . . .

'Oops!'

Edwin could *swear* Perpetua had dropped it on purpose. The pendant slipped from her fingers and bounced off Edwin's thumb. He thought fleetingly that perhaps it hadn't touched his skin for long enough, but after a few seconds his thumb began to feel warm.

'Perpetua!' Edwin yelled. 'What did you do that for?!'

'It was an accident,' she replied, not at all convincingly. Then she seemed to brace herself. She knew exactly what was about to happen. So did Edwin.

The spirit guide appeared, this time seeming to almost float into the room. Once again it turned towards

Perpetua. The soldiers drew their swords.

Edwin held up his hand. 'They're no use!' he cried. 'It's a ghost – a spirit guide . . .'

The form of the spirit began to merge into Perpetua. She cried out and Auvlin stepped forward, but Edwin held him back. 'It's happened before,' he gabbled. 'It's too late. We just have to watch . . .'

There, where Perpetua had been standing, was the spirit, once again seeming solid and almost human. The sallow skin looked real enough to touch and the trail of rope around the figure's waist swung back and forth as it took its first steps. This time the spirit didn't look only at Edwin, it looked at Auvlin too. As it inched forward, lips moving frantically, it turned its gaze from one to the other then back again. Just as before, it raised a hand to pull down its hood. The material slowly drew back.

'tic . . . tic . . . tic . . .'

The long tip of the nose was revealed.

'The spirit finds . . .'

The sharp jut of cheekbones.

'The spirit finds a . . .'

The eyes.

'The spirit finds a home!'

The eyes were open – wide open, but there was nothing to be seen. Only blackness; a deep, inky blackness staring back. There seemed to be other voices. Edwin glanced left . . . faint white mists were merging in and out of view. A hand passed in front of his face. Edwin felt an icy chill and the spirit's mouth froze, then blasted, 'THE SPIRIT FINDS A HOME!'

Edwin clasped his hands to his ears. The spirit now looked only at him. It began to shake. It came closer still. It was only inches from his face. The mouth turned up into a snarl. The body suddenly jolted.

'. . . tic . . . tic . . . tic . . .'

The snarl turned to a silent scream, the eyes creased into black slits of pain. Its hands gripped Edwin's arms. He felt it shake. It shook with anger; with fear. It took a deep, unearthly breath . . .

'THE SPIRIT FINDS A HOME!'

Edwin tried to back away. The spirit was pressing against him. Edwin could smell death. He could smell fear. He could smell magic. A hiss blasted in his ears . . .

Then, in an instant, it was gone.

Edwin looked down. Perpetua was slumped in his arms, gasping for breath.

Chapter Twelve

Perpetua hauled herself up and grabbed Edwin's shoulder. 'The spirit finds a home,' she whispered. 'Could that be me? Is it talking about *me* again?'

'I . . . I dunno,' Edwin said, closing his eyes. 'I dunno what else it could mean.' He swallowed. 'What did you go and do that for? Anything could've happened!'

Perpetua nodded. 'I know,' she said. 'That's why I did it. I thought that down here – where other ghostly things might be lurking – the spirit guide would be able to make us understand. It was only a thought.'

Edwin sighed. 'I still don't know what he's on about.' He looked at Auvlin. 'Have you got any ideas?'

The prince shook his head. 'No, nothing.' He put his

arm around Perpetua's shoulder. 'I have never seen anything like this,' he said. 'How do you feel? Do you need to sit down?'

'Yes, but not in here,' Perpetua said weakly.

'Of course,' Auvlin murmured. He scoured the ground for the relic, picked it up and compared it to the ring. 'I do not think this will help us,' he said. 'The pattern is not as similar as I thought.'

After a short discussion Edwin and Perpetua agreed. The relic was put back in its box and the ring put back on the corpse's finger. Then the soldiers pushed the lid onto the coffin and it was lifted back into place. All the while Edwin hung around at the bottom of the steps, just managing to stop himself from climbing them until the others were ready to go. When they did leave, his pace got quicker and quicker as he thought about what was behind him. He'd seen a lot in Hysteria, but that crypt was one of the scariest places he'd been.

Janus and his men didn't come back until mid-afternoon the following day. As they listened to Janus tell everyone how his journey had gone, Edwin thought that if Perpetua had to keep quiet much longer she would explode.

'We went to the house where the physician – Atolinus – lived, but the family who were there told us he had moved on many years before.'

'Could they tell you where he had gone, father?' asked Auvlin.

Janus shook his head. 'They did not know. We asked many others in the nearby village, but it seems Atolinus had not told anyone that he was leaving – not even another physician that he worked with.' He sighed. 'But someone there said he would do his best to find him for us.'

Perpetua waited a full two seconds until she blurted, 'We've got something to tell you, Your Majesty.'

The king smiled. 'I do not doubt it. I had a feeling you would all be looking for clues while we were away. What have you found?'

Auvlin had already told Perpetua that *he* would like to tell his father what had happened, so it was quite amusing for Edwin to watch her while the prince told the tale. She winced, fidgeted and pulled all sorts of faces – Edwin could see her sheer relief when the first thing Janus did was ask her a question.

'My dear Perpetua, I can only agree with Edwin. Why in the name of Hysteria did you do such a thing?' Perpetua gazed down at her hands and didn't reply, so Janus continued. 'Are you well? Has this had any lasting effect on you?'

'No, Your Majesty,' said Perpetua quietly. She looked up. 'Can you think what the spirit guide might mean?'

'Once again nothing other than what you have

yourself suggested – that it spoke of its inhabitation of you,' Janus replied.

Edwin scratched his head. 'Is Georgiara around? We wondered if her memory might be jogged by reading the notes she wrote about Leana.'

Janus ran a hand down his face. 'She has been exhausted by the journey to the north, so perhaps you should wait.' He looked up. 'Or I will talk to her myself. I already have something important to ask.'

'What is it, father?' Auvlin said.

'I cannot rest while this poor woman lives here alone, with only her delusions for company. I want to see her well again. I want to see her happy.' Janus stood up. 'I propose to take Georgiara back to Emporium Castle with us.'

'But she still doesn't know who you really are, Your Majesty,' said Perpetua.

'She will realise in time, hopefully,' Janus replied. 'Yesterday I sent word to a special consultant – I have asked him to come to the castle to assist with her recovery.'

'When do you want to go back, Your Majesty?' Bellwin asked.

'Tomorrow,' Janus replied. 'And we will leave this place looking better than we found it.'

Edwin had missed the king over the last few days. He really wanted to talk to him about the relic and was beginning to feel as if they'd never find out why it had been in the Spencer household for all those years. But Janus looked tired and before Edwin could speak to him the king went off to see Georgiara on his own.

Still, Edwin felt cheerful. This place had definitely given him the creeps and he'd be glad to leave it.

It took a day and a half to get back to Emporium Castle and they arrived to find that the 'special consultant' Janus had referred to had beaten them to it. Georgiara was taken to settle into her rooms, but Edwin, Perpetua and everyone else went straight to Ollwin's chambers, where the consultant was waiting. When they entered the room they recognised who it was straight away.

'Brolin!' Edwin said. He grinned. Wizard Brolin was one of the weirdest – but most likeable – people he'd met in all the territories.

'Oh my,' Perpetua said. But she too had to smile.

Brolin was dressed in a remarkably dirty full-length tunic and talking to – or rather *at* – Eifus and Dreifus from a distance of less than a metre. The brothers were standing against a wall as if pinned by some invisible force, their eyes wide and their mouths gaping.

'You say you are *identical* twins?' said Brolin, his mane of rats tails shaking violently. 'Did someone tell you this or have come to this conclusion yourselves?'

'Our dear departed mother said we were,' Eifus answered, in a much smaller than usual voice. 'And *she* would know better than anyone.'

'Your mother told you?' Brolin replied, his tone rising a few octaves. 'Tell me, did she suffer with bad eyesight?'

'Certainly not!' Dreifus snorted, then tried to back further into the wall.

Brolin looked from Dreifus to Eifus and stroked his straggly beard. 'I may be mistaken, but one of the criteria for qualifying as identical twins is being, in fact, identical.'

'Yes?' the brothers said together. Then they seemed to hold their breath.

'Well . . .' Brolin replied, completely oblivious that anyone else had entered the room. He tutted, took a step forward and stood on tiptoe to put his hand on Eifus's head. He waited a moment, then slowly brought this hand down the steep trajectory to Dreifus's head. The brothers glanced at each other, then both looked blankly at Brolin. The wizard put his hand back up to Eifus then down to Dreifus, then up and down and up and down like a 1980s disco dancer. Finally he seemed to run out of patience. Eifus and Dreifus continued to stare at him, apparently oblivious to what he was trying to say.

'Brolin!' Janus said suddenly. The wizard jumped, but quickly recovered himself and turned around with a smile.

'Your Majesty,' he said, scuttling forward. 'I was just having a most interesting discussion with these two gentlemen.' He glanced around at Eifus and Dreifus, then said out of the corner of his mouth, 'They think they are identical twins. Are you aware of this?'

'Yes,' Janus replied in hushed tones. 'I think *everyone* in Emporium Castle is aware.'

Brolin raised his eyebrows. 'With the greatest respect, Sire,' he whispered, 'is it wise to have delusional courtiers in attendance?' He didn't wait for an answer. 'I once treated a farmer who was sure he was married to his prize breeding pig. He would introduce her to complete strangers as "my dear, dear wife". Their happiness, however, was short lived – when she gave birth to piglets he disowned her.'

'Why?' Bellwin said, open mouthed.

'He said they looked nothing like him.'

Edwin and Perpetua smothered giggles and Brolin looked at them. Of course he had no idea who they really were. 'Lady Perpetua,' Brolin said grandly. 'And . . .' But as he glanced at Auvlin he stopped. 'Forgive me, but I am confused, Your Majesty,' he said to Janus. 'You appear to have two heirs to your throne – one slightly older than the other.'

Janus smiled. 'Of course, you have not heard Edwin and Perpetua's *real* story. Perhaps we should explain before we do anything else.'

They all sat down and Brolin was told everything. Everyone joined in to tell the tale and by the end of it the wizard looked quite overwhelmed. 'That is the strangest thing I have ever heard,' he said, shaking his head. He looked at Edwin. 'I remember the first time I saw you, I said you had the look of royalty.' He blinked. 'And I was so sure'

Everyone looked at Edwin, who felt his cheeks stain red. He felt like a bit of a fraud.

'Now, Wizard Brolin,' said Janus firmly. 'We have brought you here to help us.'

'Yes, yes, of course,' Brolin replied eagerly. 'What can I do for you?'

'We have brought the cousin of the late Queen Ahven to Emporium Castle. The poor woman suffered the loss of three close family members within a short time and it has disturbed her mind.'

'Bit of an understatement,' Edwin muttered to Perpetua. 'She's as mad as a box of frogs.' Perpetua shot him a look.

'But she is not at all dangerous,' Janus continued. 'Georgiara is, and has always been, a kind and gentle soul.'

'I see,' Brolin said quietly. 'And you would like me to cure this lady?'

'Yes,' Janus said anxiously. 'If you can.'

Edwin studied Janus. He knew the king was caring, but he seemed really worried about Georgiara.

'Well I can only try my best, Your Majesty,' Brolin said. 'It will be an honour to serve you again.'

'Thank you my friend,' Janus replied, getting to his

feet. 'We will of course pay you generously. Would you like to eat with Auvlin, Edwin and Perpetua this evening? I need to meet with my courtiers.'

'Yes, that would be very pleasant, Sire,' Brolin said. 'And perhaps my dear friend Bellwin, too?'

Bellwin grinned. 'That would be marvellous.'

Janus looked pleased. 'Very good,' he said. 'I shall leave you to find your bearings, Brolin. Perhaps we can meet in the morning . . . I will bring Georgiara with me.'

'Of course.'

The king left Ollwin's chambers and Brolin turned to Edwin. 'The wonder that is Emporium Castle . . . tales of strange other worlds . . . marvellous adventure stories. What a treat this is for humble Wizard Brolin!'

Brolin was so excited by his new surroundings that Edwin had decided not to warn him about the castle's food. But when it came to it the meal they were served was really quite nice. All five were very hungry, so it was no time at all until the proper conversation could begin.

'How is your practice, Brolin?' Bellwin asked, pushing his plate to one side. 'I expect you were busy again after this year's great feasting?'

Brolin threw his head back. 'My dear, dear friend,' he said dramatically. 'The over-indulgence was worse than ever. I treated one man who has now come to me *nine years running*. Every year I tell him to resist the greenacre sprouts, resist the buttered turnip mash, *resist* the lemon-and-cream pastry pie.' Brolin closed his eyes and shook his head disapprovingly. 'But he does not listen. His wife confided in me that the venting of his wind could be heard seven dwellings along. A very unsavoury affair.'

Everyone else sat in silence for a while. Edwin decided they were all trying to picture what Brolin had described. 'Sounds like he could have broken some kind of record there,' he said thoughtfully, and then suddenly smiled. 'Ha! Broke . . . wind. It's a joke!'

'Edwin, please don't dwell on bodily functions,' Perpetua snapped. 'We have far more important things to think about.'

Edwin smothered his grin.

Auvlin turned to Brolin. 'Was it an inconvenience to be summoned here?'

'No, not at all. There was nothing that needed my urgent attention.' Brolin tilted his head. 'Can you tell me anything about Georgiara?'

They told Brolin what little they knew about the queen's cousin. He listened intently.

'Did you know that she was ill?' he asked. 'Is that why you went to Jozeponi?'

'We didn't have a clue,' Perpetua answered. 'We were trying to find out something about a relic that belonged to Queen Ahven, Janus's late wife, and Jozeponi is where she came from.'

'Yeah, it's all a bit weird,' Edwin added. 'Ahven's grandmother Leana gave her this relic and somehow it ended up in my house on Earth, just after I was born.'

'A relic that has travelled between worlds! I have never heard of that before,' Brolin murmured. 'Can you tell me what it looks like?'

'Why, we can do better than that,' Auvlin replied, looking at Edwin. 'We can show it to you.'

Edwin fumbled in his pocket, brought out the box and opened it. 'Here it is. It's called the Sceptre of Jozeponi.'

Brolin looked at the relic. 'I hoped I would recognise it, but I do not.'

'Can't say I'm surprised,' said Edwin flatly. 'We can't find out much about it from anywhere. *Ancient Relics of These Territories* only told us it was made in Jozeponi.'

'Can I pick it up?' Brolin asked.

Edwin nodded. He was now convinced he was the only person who could make the spirit guide appear.

Brolin took the sceptre from the box and examined it closely. 'These tiny patterns at the end,' he said thoughtfully. 'They mean something.'

'Mean something?' Bellwin repeated, leaning in to have a better look.

Brolin squinted. 'Patterns such as these – etched on jewellery, relics, portrait frames – they are symbolic . . . they have meaning.'

'Like a language?' Perpetua asked. She turned to Edwin. 'That would be a bit like hieroglyphics in Ancient Egypt.'

Auvlin touched Brolin's arm. 'Are you able to translate them?'

'Not without a spell, my friend.' Brolin twisted the sceptre between his fingers. He closed his eyes, as if he were thinking hard. 'I remember using a charm many years ago. It gave the translation of an intricate drawing that a woman in a nearby village found on her door.'

'That sounds a bit sinister,' Edwin whispered. 'Was it drawn in blood?'

'Oh, no,' Brolin replied brightly. 'It was not sinister at all. It was in fact a proposal of marriage. I used the spell and was able to tell the good lady what the drawing meant.' His face fell. 'But she misunderstood and thought I was asking her to marry *me*.'

Edwin turned down his mouth. 'What happened?'

'She ran away before I could explain that it was someone else who had asked for her hand.'

Perpetua couldn't look at any of the others, but she managed to disguise a laugh with a cough. 'So, er . . . can you still perform this spell?'

'Of course. Once I have performed a charm it is with me forever.'

'What are we waiting for, then?' Edwin cried. 'Let's do it!'

Brolin looked down. 'Very well,' he said. 'I will need

something hard . . . a stone or a piece of wood.'

'I'll get it!' Perpetua blurted. 'I'll go to the kitchen!' She bolted from the table and in no time at all was back brandishing a wooden spoon.

Brolin took it and sat up straight. 'Now, I need to trace the pattern onto a surface – this table will do. I will not draw as such, I need only to copy the shapes with this implement.'

The wizard peered closely at the sceptre then placed the spoon's handle on the table. He began to move it, curling, circling, tracing out delicate flourishes at the corners. He began to poke his tongue out in concentration and by the time he'd finished its tip was almost touching the end of his nose.

'That will be sufficient.' Brolin put the spoon down and held out his hands with his fingers spread wide. 'Scriberius ashine,' he said softly. Almost at once the pattern he had copied glowed bright white on the table.

'Wow!' said Edwin. 'That's amazing!'

'What does it say?' Perpetua hissed, getting straight to the point.

'One moment, please,' said Brolin imperiously. He parted his lips and began to breathe in. As he did so the pattern's light began to drift upwards, seeping through the air towards his face. He expanded his chest and the light streaked into his mouth and out of sight. Brolin blinked hard and swallowed.

'Yes . . . the pattern does have meaning,' he said,

looking slightly stunned.

Edwin leaned in and held his breath.

'If someone holds the sceptre in their clenched fist for more than three minutes, it is able to tell them their date of birth . . . and the date on which they will die.' Brolin looked around the table as if he could barely believe what he'd just said.

Edwin's mouth fell open and Perpetua's eyes were wide. 'The date on which they'd die,' she repeated. 'Who on Earth – or Hysteria – would want to know *that*?

At first Edwin nodded in agreement, but then he started to think about it. 'You know, I reckon quite a lot of people *would* want to find out. They'd want to know, hoping they'd be told that they've got ages to live.'

Perpetua paused, then shook her head. 'But what if they were told they *didn't* have ages to live? They'd be distraught. They'd go mad. I'd rather not know and just get on with living.'

'But not everyone is as disciplined as you,' said Bellwin. 'I think I would *try* to resist, but that knowledge would be a great temptation.'

'I'm with you on that,' Edwin said. 'It's like having a bar of chocolate in your school bag. If you don't know it's there, you don't think about it. If you find it halfway through double maths, all you wanna do is eat it.'

Perpetua's mouth twitched. 'Well, I can see how *some* people might be tempted. But, more interestingly, we now know for sure the "other means" used by Leanna to find out her date of birth.'

Bellwin looked at Brolin. 'You said the relic also gave the day of death. I wonder if Leana also found out when she was going to die?'

'From what you just said, Brolin,' Edwin interrupted, 'it sounds like it gave both whether or not it was wanted.' He frowned. 'I wonder what made Leana give it to Ahven, though?'

Then Edwin's stomach lurched. He looked across at Auvlin and saw that the prince had turned very pale.

'Do you realise what this means,' Auvlin whispered. 'My mother could have used the sceptre to find out the day that she would die.' He hesitated, as if trying to process his thoughts. 'When she was pregnant with me and went to Jozeponi, did she know full well that she would never return to Emporium Castle?'

Perpetua reached over to touch Auvlin's hand. 'The queen may not have used the relic herself,' she said softly. 'Don't jump to any conclusions. But what we need to do is tell the king all this . . . '

Auvlin scraped a hand back through his hair. 'No. We must not do that,' he said, his voice quivering. 'I fear it would break his heart. My father's most precious memories are of his years spent with my mother. Why should I trouble him with this? If the relic had not been disturbed this puzzle would never had presented itself.'

Edwin looked down. This was his fault. Why did he have to go sorting through all that baby stuff? 'I'm sorry,' he murmured. 'I shouldn't have picked the sceptre up.'

Auvlin blinked, then leant forward to grasp Edwin's arm. 'You were not to know, dear friend,' he said. Edwin looked back up and his gaze met Auvlin's. For that moment, that brief, fleeting moment, something was exchanged between them.

'I think Auvlin's right,' Edwin said suddenly. 'It would be a horrible thing for Janus to hear.' He looked at Brolin. 'If what you've told us takes the mystery anywhere, we need to sort it out on our own. If we *have* to tell him later, we do it then.'

Brolin nodded. 'You and Auvlin know Janus much better than I.' He thought for a while. 'The next question that springs to mind, Edwin, is why and how did the relic came to be in your home?'

Edwin nodded. 'Yeah, exactly. It's not like my parents would even have a clue what it was for. And why would it end up in my cot in hospital the day after I was born?' All was quiet and Edwin added, 'This is gonna take some thinking about.'

Perpetua nodded, then glanced at Auvlin. His head was in his hands and he looked as if he was fighting tears. She quickly changed the subject.

'Brolin, when you start treating Georgiara, can I come and watch?'

'I'd like to as well,' Edwin added, glad that Perpetua had filled the silence.

'I will not come,' Auvlin blurted. 'I have some things

to attend to.'

Brolin patted the prince's hand. 'Any of you that wish to watch me at work may do so.' He smiled at Bellwin. 'Your presence will no doubt stir my blood to produce an even better performance. Come to my room tomorrow morning, straight after breakfast and prepare to be enlightened.'

CHAPTER THIRTEEN

JANUS WAS ALREADY THERE THE following morning when everyone arrived in Brolin's room and Georgiara's treatment had begun. But Brolin offered no apologies. 'A king is in attendance and I cannot delay when inspiration strikes,' he declared.

They all took a seat except Perpetua, who stood right beside the patient. 'How are you, Georgiara?' she asked.

Georgiara smiled. 'I feel a little different already,' she said slowly. 'I think I have not been myself for many years. I am trying to remember certain things . . .'

Brolin held up his hand. 'Do not try too much at this point,' he said gently. 'You must let the spell take its course.'

'So are we finished, sir?' Georgiara asked.

'Not quite, my dear.' Brolin picked up a bag from his lap and took out a small green leaf. He whispered something, then blew on the leaf and within a few moments it began to gradually disappear. The few centimetres around its shrinking outline became distorted, like an image in a fairground mirror, and the distortion began to seep from one side towards Georgiara.

'Close your eyes,' Brolin instructed.

Georgiara did as she was told and her expression seemed to relax as the as the narrow ripple of light reached her face. It took a few minutes for the leaf to fade completely. When it had, Brolin clicked his fingers and Georgiara came to as if she'd been in a hypnotic trance. Her skin was a little brighter and her eyes didn't look quite so strained.

'How are you now – do you feel well?' Janus said, leaning forward.

'Oh, yes,' replied Georgiara. 'My mind feels a little clearer all the time.' She looked closely at the king. 'Janus. *Janus*,' she murmured. 'Sir, I am more and more sure we met *before* you came to my house . . .'

Brolin looked at the king and nodded. 'Now, my dear Georgiara,' he said. 'We have made an excellent start, but there is more treatment to come. Now, I insist that you rest for the remainder of the day.'

Georgiara stood up and Janus quickly did the same.

'I will walk with you to your room,' he said kindly. 'You may be a little unsteady on your feet.' He took Georgiara's hand and they walked slowly out of the door. Edwin watched them until they disappeared from sight. Janus looked different from how he'd ever seen him before.

'Well, well, well,' Brolin said brightly. 'That took very little time. What shall we do for the rest of the day?'

Edwin brightened. 'I know we've got a lot to think about, but would you like a tour of the castle? I know my way around really well.'

Perpetua was obviously feeling generous. 'Yes, he *really* does.'

'I can think of nothing better,' Brolin chimed. 'But first I require some exercise!' He rose from his seat and started to perform some kind of dance, as if he were ringing church bells whilst stepping on hot coals.

'You really gotta hand it to him,' Edwin said to Perpetua. 'He just doesn't care.'

Brolin did this dance for around thirty seconds then finished with a star jump. 'Ah, what it is to be an athlete,' he said, wiping his brow. 'Shall we begin our tour, dear friends?'

Edwin was in his element as the castle tour guide. And it was even better when it was someone like Brolin. The wizard had marvelled at the Great Hall, gasped at the armoury and in the kitchen drove the cook to distraction by asking about every single meal she'd ever made. 'And how long would that take to eat?' he asked at one point, to which the cook replied firmly, 'It depends how big the mouth.'

This all seemed to put Brolin in an even more cheerful than usual mood, so Edwin was quite surprised when the wizard said he'd like to see the mausoleum.

Edwin began to feel slightly shivery as they made their way down to the depths of the castle. When they reached the mausoleum he was glad to see that, just as before, two torches were flaming either side of the arched wooden door. A few years ago the room had always been locked by order of Janus, but when Brolin tried the door, it swung open.

The room was not lit up – meaning, thankfully, that it was not in use. Brolin took several steps in, but Edwin and Perpetua hung back near the doorway. The stone plinth in the middle of the room was in partial shadow and at once Edwin recalled the sight of Auvlin lying there, his resting place hung with garlands of yellow flowers. He could remember vividly the first time he'd seen that perfect reflection of himself in that cold, still body.

'What made you want to see this?' he said.

Brolin gazed around the room. 'Shadow Magic, my friend. What happened here has gone down in legend as the most audacious spell attempted by the Umbrians

– to instil the spirit of the dead Hereticus in Auvlin's body.' He looked quickly from corner to corner. 'Ollwin has told me the dark auras were banished, but a faint echo will always remain. I can feel it.'

Edwin swallowed. 'You know that the spirit just vanished, don't you?' he said. 'And no one knows where it went . . .'

'How can a spirit think and feel without a body?' Perpetua said, almost to herself. 'Is it aware of other spirits . . . do they communicate with each other?'

Brolin looked at Perpetua. 'These are questions that cannot be answered.' He looked through the mausoleum door to the passage outside. 'I can feel other troubles in this castle,' he continued. 'Apart from the relic and lady Georgiara, there is some other issue concerning the court. Am I right?'

Edwin bit his lip. Should he tell Brolin? Well, why not? The wizard had done nothing but help Hysteria in the past.

'Yeah, there is something,' Edwin said slowly. 'And I reckon Janus wouldn't mind if I told you.'

'I don't think so either,' Perpetua said.

'Well,' Brolin said, stepping a little further into the light. 'Please do.'

'What . . . tell you about it here?' said Edwin reluctantly. The mausoleum may have been missing a dead body, but it was still the creepiest place in the castle.

Brolin nodded. 'No time like the present, my friend.'

Once again Perpetua couldn't let Edwin tell the tale on his own and it wasn't very long before Brolin knew all about the skeletons in the cave and what they'd turned out to be. They also told him about the discovery, a year ago, that much of Umbria's army was made up of the very same clones.

Brolin was intrigued. 'That is fascinating. Umbrian clone remains on Hysterian territory – it is no wonder Janus is concerned. But why were they hidden and chained? What possible purpose would that serve?'

'Yeah,' Edwin agreed. 'That's what we're all trying to find out.'

'Brolin,' said Perpetua said, 'you know how the Umbrians use transformation – is that similar to how they make clones? Changing one person into the image of another?'

'Why, no,' Brolin replied. 'As you might remember, transformation uses only a small sample of body tissue – a hair, a fingernail – and the changes are purely physical. The transformed person may *look* like someone else, but they still retain their own thoughts.'

'So what's the difference with clones?' Edwin said.

'Well, there we have a *complete* replication. They are a physical, mental and spiritual copy and the entire original is required every single time.'

Edwin scratched his head. 'The clones in the Umbrian army were physically strong,' he said. 'But they didn't seem to have a mind of their own, and all they wanted to do was fight the enemy.'

'It must have taken a long time to find someone like that,' Perpetua said. 'I wonder who the original is. And where do they keep him?'

Suddenly, Edwin's thoughts were leaping ahead. 'The existence of this man – whoever he is – strengthens Umbria's army, doesn't he?'

'Yes. Of course,' Perpetua replied. 'Those clones are a force to be reckoned with by *anyone*.'

Edwin held up his hands. Suddenly he felt very excited. 'So I'm thinking that if someone found the man the Umbrians clone from and killed him, it would do some serious damage.'

Brolin nodded. 'From what you have told me, Edwin – it would, without question.'

Edwin looked back at the marble plinth. He visualised Janus standing there, crying over Auvlin's body. He remembered Mersium kneeling in the Throne Room . . . ready for an Umbrian execution. He thought of the constant threat: Umbria wanted to rule Hysteria, no matter how many lives they took.

'I want to get the original man,' Edwin said slowly. 'I want to get him and stop the Umbrians – stop what they're doing.'

Perpetua's eyes widened. 'Do you, Edwin. Do you really?' She swallowed as if she couldn't believe what she was about to say. 'Me too.'

Brolin looked from Perpetua to Edwin, his eyes bright. He threaded his fingers. 'Who could resist such a noble thought? He or she who defeats Umbria will liberate Hysteria – will liberate us all – from centuries of fear.'

Edwin felt the pit of his stomach twinge. 'Will you help us, Brolin?' he said.

One corner of Brolin's mouth turned up into a faint smile. 'Of course, my friend.'

Perpetua almost jumped up and down. 'What do we do first?' she asked. 'How do we find him?'

Brolin thought for a moment. 'These men are mindless, fearless and vicious. The original may well be someone who is well known within Umbria. He may have been found in the Umbrian army itself.' He stroked his beard. 'Is there anyone or anything in the castle that might help us to look into this?'

Without seemingly a moment's thought, Perpetua blurted, 'Tivoli!'

Brolin frowned. 'Tivoli?' he repeated. 'And who is he or she, dear lady?'

'*She* is the Keeper of the Relics. Janus took us to see her. She's really well read. When we met her she was reading a history of all the wars that had ever been fought here. *She* might know – she may even still have the book.'

'Bit of a long shot,' Edwin said. 'It might not even mention anything about it.'

'Yes,' Perpetua agreed. 'But still worth it.'

'This could be promising,' Brolin said. 'Can you take me to her?'

'Small problem,' Edwin replied. 'We don't know the password.'

But Perpetua shook her head. She had the look that said she'd come up with a particularly brilliant idea, even for her. 'Well, I think I may be able to guess it . . .'

They stood in the darkened passage outside the secret tower. Edwin shivered. Every time they'd been here he was sure they were going to get caught. Brolin, however, was crazy with excitement. Edwin couldn't see him properly, but he could hear the wizard's scuffling feet and rapid breathing.

'This is so unexpected,' Brolin hissed. 'I will have so much to write in my diary when I return to Meticulla!'

'Are you going to try then, Perpetua?' Edwin said. 'The longer we hang around the more chance we have of being found out.' He took Perpetua's hand and led her up the steps. 'Go on, get on with it!'

Perpetua took a deep breath and mumbled something that Edwin thought sounded familiar.

'Did you just say *Rihanna*?'

'No I did not!' Perpetua snapped.

'Who, may I ask, is Rihanna?' said Brolin.

'She's a singer . . . on Earth,' Perpetua replied. 'But we

really don't want to get into that now. I'm going to try another '

'Is it Beyoncé?' said Edwin.

'Patience . . . patience,' Brolin said softly. 'Let the young lady try again.'

There was another pause. Perpetua said, 'Garuder.'

Edwin was about the ask what on earth she was on about, but the wall in front of them suddenly started to disappear brick by brick, the light into the passage steadily increasing. The process finished with a welcome *Boom*.

'I've done it!' Perpetua cried. 'We're in!'

'Yeah, well done,' Edwin said vaguely. 'But what *was* that you said?'

'Minimianna Garuder!' Perpetua said brightly.

'Who? What? Where?'

'Tivoli's favourite author . . . Minimianna Garuder. Remember? I guessed that one of her names would be the password into the tower.'

Edwin studied Perpetua, then narrowed his eyes. 'That's good,' he said. 'That's really, really good.'

Edwin and Perpetua stepped over the threshold into the tower and told Brolin to follow. He stood looking at the ground way below for a few seconds, then they each took a hand and pulled him into the room.

'By Meticulla!' Brolin said, staring back into the partial darkness of the passage. 'What a marvellous example of Hysterian magic!'

They quickly passed into the room where Tivoli was. She looked surprised to see them as they hurried in and sat down on the floor.

'Good morning. Janus is not with you?' said Tivoli, putting down a book.

'No. Not today,' Perpetua said carefully.

'Is that a problem?' Brolin whispered to Edwin.

He shook his head. 'Nah. The last Keeper of the Relics told us they're not allowed to repeat anything about the conversations they have in here – not to anyone. Nobody is gonna find out we've been here.'

'Ah, I see.' Brolin pointed a finger in the air.

'How are you?' Perpetua asked Tivoli.

'I am well. And you?'

'Oh, we're great,' Edwin replied cheerfully. 'This is Wizard Brolin, from Meticulla. He's here to help King Janus. We've, er . . . we've come to ask you something.'

'What's that you're reading?' Perpetua asked hopefully. 'Is it the same book as before?'

'Oh, no,' Tivoli replied. 'This is a something quite different. It is the story of King Janus the seventy-fourth's attempt to reorganise the running of the castle. It took many, many years.'

Edwin raised his eyebrows. 'Sounds unputdownable.'

'Oh, that's a shame,' Perpetua said. 'We need to find out something and the other book might have helped us.'

'I have an excellent memory,' Tivoli said. 'Ask me a

question – I may know the answer.'

Perpetua coughed and shifted on the floor. 'The book you were reading was about all the wars in the territories, wasn't it? Well, we wondered if it mentioned a particular soldier in the Umbrian army?'

'What was the name of this man?' Tivoli asked.

'I'm afraid we don't know. What we do know is he was very tall and strong and he was, well, he was almost mindless – totally fearless. All he thought about was killing the enemy.'

Tivoli stared at Perpetua and slowly shook her head. 'This man did not fight for Umbria –'

Perpetua's shoulders slumped.

'– he was taken into the army, but he was too dangerous.'

'You do know of him then!' Edwin cried.

'Too dangerous?' Perpetua said. 'How could a soldier be *too dangerous*?'

'Listen and you will see quite clearly,' Tivoli replied. 'The book mentions a young man – not by name – who lived in a village not far from the borders of Umbria. He was very strong, but simple-minded. He was taken into the army, but he was too reckless and he would often attack fellow soldiers. Once set on killing, it was impossible to stop him. When he was returned to his village he killed many members of other families. The village elders wanted him to be executed, but the leaders of the Umbrian army decided to once again take him away from his home – this time out of sight.'

'That *has* to be the original for the clones. Do you know where he was taken?' Perpetua asked.

'I am afraid the book did not say.'

Edwin turned to Perpetua. 'It's gotta be the Umbrian villa, where they performed the transformations. That's where all the child clones were.'

Perpetua gazed back at him. 'Absolutely – it'd make sense to keep them in the same place as the original.'

'Let's go and find out!' Edwin said, jumping to his feet. 'Janus can bring his whole army. We know exactly what this bloke looks like.'

'There's a big *but*,' said Perpetua. 'There might be quite a few men in the villa who look just like him. We won't know which one is the original.'

'But they started cloning him when he was an adult,' Edwin replied. 'All the clones have had to grow up, so none of them are going to look as old as *him*.'

Perpetua shook her head. 'But what if some of the clones look much older than they really are. The Umbrians may have experimented on them . . . they could have done anything. And the original has been subjected to Shadow Magic – that may have changed *him*.'

'Wait,' Brolin interrupted. 'Tivoli – do you happen to know how old this man would be now?'

Tivoli thought for a moment. 'He would be forty six.'

'Then you know his date of birth?' Perpetua asked.

'He was born on a day sacred to the Umbrians. It was one reason why he was not executed by the army.'

Edwin looked from Brolin to Perpetua. 'Then there *is* a way to be sure we get the right person . . . it's absolutely fool-proof!'

'I think I know what you are going to say, Edwin,' Brolin said with a smile.

Perpetua gave a little whimper. 'So do I! The Sceptre of Jozeponi can tell someone when they are going to die . . . and *when they were born*.' Her fist thumped the floor. 'It's perfect!'

Edwin didn't have time to enjoy the moment. 'Tivoli – could you write down the date for us?'

'Yes, of course.' Tivoli went to the ante chamber and came back a few moments later.

The piece of paper she handed to Edwin had a series of numbers written on it that made no sense to him, but Bellwin and Auvlin would know what the meant.

'Thanks,' he said. 'You've been a lot of help.'

Perpetua leant over to shake Tivoli's hand. 'I don't think we'd have got any further without you.'

'I am glad to be of service,' Tivoli replied. 'Are there any other questions for me?'

Edwin got to his feet and pulled Perpetua up. 'No, ta, we'd better go.'

'My lady,' Brolin said, looking in wonder around the room. 'I would dearly love to spend many hours with you in discussion. But alas I am here to help my friends, and I must leave.' He threw back his rat tails and gave Tivoli a warm smile.

'I understand,' Tivoli said. 'It is possible we will meet again?'

'I do hope so, dear lady. It would be a pleasure.' He got up, turned on his heel and made for the door. 'I return to our task,' he whispered to Edwin. 'My heart is enraptured, but I must resist.'

Once out in the passage, Perpetua said 'Garuder' and the wall rebuilt itself in less than a minute. They scuttled out into the dim light of the gallery.

'So,' Edwin said. 'This original man. We probably know where to look, we *definitely* know how to make sure it's him.'

'I wonder if Janus still has the stuff that got us into the Umbrian villa before?' said Perpetua.

Edwin sighed and ran his hand though his hair. 'We're gonna have to do this without Janus. If he comes with us, he'll find out what the relic is for . . . '

Perpetua touched Edwin's arm. 'Are you sure you don't want him to know? Is it not worth telling him?'

'Yeah. Didn't you see Auvlin's face? He knows Janus would be devastated if he thought that Ahven went away to die.'

Perpetua nodded. 'Yes,' she said softly. 'I'm sure you're right.'

'We have to decide our course of action,' Brolin said. 'Do you have any suggestions?'

'First we tell Auvlin,' Perpetua answered. 'Then we'll decide.' She looked at Edwin. 'Do you think he'll want to go to the fort? D'you think he'll want to find and kill this man?'

'You're joking, right?' Edwin replied. "Course he will. And so do I.'

Chapter Fourteen

Edwin and Perpetua managed to find Auvlin very quickly, and Edwin was proved right. It was obvious before they'd even finished telling the prince what had happened that he wanted to go to the Umbrian villa as soon as he could.

Auvlin sent for Bellwin and asked him if he'd join them. Of course, the young wizard said yes; he too agreed that they should go without the king's knowledge. They decided they would leave early the next morning. Delius and Brolin would cover for them all as long as they possibly could, and hopefully by the time anyone noticed they had gone they should be well on their way to Umbria.

The morning arrived, but it was still dark as they led their horses through a narrow gap in the castle gate. Edwin felt uneasy about going to the Umbrian villa without Janus, but it would be worth it if they could find and kill the man Tivoli had told them about. But one thing really worried him – when they'd gone to the Umbrian villa before they'd had the entire King's Guard with them. This time they only numbered four. And one of them was Perpetua.

They travelled for over twelve hours and set up camp just as night was falling. They ate, discussed what they'd do the next day, and very soon they were all asleep. Edwin slept pretty soundly, but still told Perpetua the following morning that she'd snored all night.

They set off early again and crossed the Umbrian border in under an hour. They tied up their horses about a kilometre from the villa. As they approached it, light barely creeping into the sky, Edwin wished they'd taken at least one or two soldiers with them. He checked that he still had the Sceptre of Jozeponi in his pocket.

'Now, let us go over our plan again,' said Auvlin. 'I will lead us through the villa and will talk to the guards or anyone else if necessary. I think we should try the cells first.'

'It is the best place to start,' said Bellwin.

'Definitely,' Edwin agreed. 'But, er, what if this man isn't there?'

Auvlin paused then shook his head slowly. 'I do not know, Edwin.'

The villa came into full view and everyone pulled up their hoods and tried to stand as tall as they could. Edwin squinted at the torchlit doorway and felt his stomach twinge. A guard the size of a mountain stood between them and the villa. Two swords hung from his belt and something else glinted in his hand. He was armed to the teeth.

Auvlin was easily the biggest of them and everyone let him stride in front as the villa came closer.

'Huma guana man,' Auvlin shouted out, his voice much deeper than usual.

'Huma guana,' the guard replied. Auvlin came to a stop and held up his hand. The guard looked at him closely, then stepped down the line to examine them all. Edwin was tugged forward as the guard looked under his hood and his heart began to thump.

'Guana,' the guard grunted at Edwin. 'Why are you here?'

'We have urgent business with Wizard Hadius,' said Auvlin loudly. 'He is expecting *this*.' He held up a glass phial which was filled with a thick brown liquid.

The man stomped back. 'Let me see,' he snapped. He took the phial from Auvlin and unplugged the stopper.

'It is harmless . . . to Umbrians,' Auvlin said pointedly.

The guard huffed. 'And to Hysterians?'

'It means death,' Auvlin said, as lightly as he could.

The guard took a tiny sniff, then wrinkled his nose. He waited, perhaps to see if anything happened. When it didn't, he looked at each one of them and then knocked on the door three times. It swung open and the guard said, 'Enter!'

It was only when they'd passed through into the villa that Edwin realised how hot he was. The cloak suddenly felt like a fur coat, but he didn't want to pull his hood down. They could see *anyone* in here – someone who might recognise him as the king's heir. Sort of.

Bellwin helped Auvlin navigate the route to the cells they'd visited before, the two of them moving quickly and quietly and mostly using only gestures to show the way. When Auvlin did speak his voice was slightly shaky, and Edwin guessed that coming back here must be pretty hard.

Two men suddenly appeared around a corner. Edwin felt Perpetua's arm tense alongside his. He tried not to grimace as he held his breath, but the men ignored them and brushed past without a glance.

Auvlin led them to a stairwell. It was very cold and Edwin could feel the beads of sweat on his face begin to cool. They descended one flight, went straight on and turned into a passage to the right, then on past a line of portraits towards a wooden door. It was eerily quiet.

Auvlin opened the door and they filed quickly through.

'Yes, this is the place,' Perpetua said, looking around

the hexagonal room. As before, the walls were lined with large jars containing human organs and an examination table stood in the middle.

'They're still up to no good,' Edwin said.

The door leading to the cells was unlocked and everyone slipped through. They were standing at the top of a dimly lit passage.

'I was kept here,' said Auvlin, 'about halfway down. I did not see what lay beyond it.'

'We didn't get that far either,' said Edwin.

'Let us look!' interrupted Bellwin. 'We are wasting time!'

The four figures walked down the passage, each glancing from side to side. The familiar figures of cloned children sat dozens to a cell, very still and very silent. They didn't look up. They made no sound. Edwin swallowed. It seemed nothing had changed here at all.

Auvlin slowed his pace outside one of the cells and Edwin assumed it had been his. The cell was empty now. As they came to the next one, Edwin started to brace himself. Any second he expected a giant of a man to come rushing at the bars, baring his teeth, rage in his eyes. But that cell was unoccupied, too. And the one opposite, and the one after that . . . two, three, four . . .

Then everyone stopped dead. The very last cell in the line was occupied by five men. They were all clones.

One was chained to the wall. There was a tube in his arm that trailed to the floor and at the end was a small puddle of blood. The man was very still and much paler than the rest. Edwin's thoughts flashed back to the cave, to the holes in the wall. Then he heard Brolin, talking about Shadow Magic: *hundreds of years ago they found a way to evade the curse – quite simply, they drink the blood of other humans . . .*

'That's what the clones were in the cave for,' Perpetua said, taking the words out of Edwin's mouth. 'Two years ago, when the Umbrians captured Emporium Castle, they were going to be a blood supply for wizards practising Shadow Magic.' She shook her head. 'It's . . . it's barbaric.'

Edwin couldn't take his eyes from the clone body. This was an Umbrian. This was what they did to each other. But Auvlin suddenly shook him. 'This is a truly terrible sight,' he said. 'But we do not have time to dwell on it. The man we need is not here.'

'Yeah. Sure.' Edwin roused himself. 'Then where *is* he?' He put his hands to his head. Suddenly his thoughts were no more than a muddle. Where else could they look? Was the man at the Umbrian fort? What *were* they going to do?

'Bellwin,' Perpetua said suddenly. 'You know the spell where you're able to tune someone's mind into a particular voice and help them locate it – can you do that here?'

'I could, Perpetua, but what if the soldier clones do not talk because the *original* does not talk. There will be nothing to focus on.'

'Well . . .' Perpetua added slowly. 'What if we ask for the sound of his breathing? He *will* breathe, won't he!'

Bellwin shrugged but said, 'I can try an adaptation. But there is one more problem – we do not know the man's name.'

'Is there any other way we can refer to him?' Perpetua said.

'Crikey!' said Edwin. 'Now that *is* a tough one. Umbrian mentalist? Big strong Umbrian man?'

'Don't be stupid, Edwin,' Perpetua sighed.

'But think –' said Auvlin suddenly. 'Tivoli said he came from a village near the Umbrian border. She *must* mean the border with Hysteria. We crossed it only a short while ago. Which villages were near?'

'Oh . . . er . . .' Perpetua said, screwing up her eyes. 'Sorlo . . . Soro . . . ?'

'Sorlon!' Auvlin hissed. 'There were two others to the west. One was Enersh, but the other, I cannot remember.'

Edwin grimaced. 'Me neither. But shall we try the other two? Bellwin, try the spell, but instead of "voice" say "breathing" and instead of a name say "man from Sorlon". Apart from that everything is the same.'

Bellwin sighed. 'It could hardly be more different. I am not at all sure the spell will work.'

'Just try,' Perpetua insisted. 'We'll see what happens.

Edwin, d'you want to be the one to hear it?'

Edwin wasn't sure, but he nodded. He stood in front of Bellwin. The wizard frowned and raised his left hand. 'Inhalium tunertarium . . . masculine ata Sorlon.'

Edwin held his breath and waited for the sound. After what seemed like an age he closed his eyes – maybe that would help. But there was still nothing. He opened one eye. 'It didn't work. Let's try the other one.'

Bellwin shook his head. 'I hold out very little hope for this,' he murmured. But he stood in the same position and said, 'Inhalium tunetarium . . . masculine ata Enersh.'

Edwin stood bolt upright almost at once. There was the sound of heavy, grating breathing in his head. It was almost a growl. 'Er, got something,' he said weakly. 'It ain't exactly a purr.'

'But does it sound like you might expect?' Perpetua asked.

'Crikey, yeah!'

'Can you tell where it's coming from?' Auvlin said eagerly.

Edwin looked around. 'It's above us. I think on the next floor.'

'Then follow me. We must hurry.'

Edwin and the others turned and followed Auvlin along the passage. It was strange – Edwin could hear the others but their voices were muffled under the breathing that dominated his hearing. Auvlin traced their way back to the spiralling steps, then peered upwards. He nodded and then started to climb them. Soon they reached the next floor. It was pretty dark.

'Which way?' Auvlin hissed.

Edwin blinked. 'Left,' he answered. 'It's not far from here.'

This time Edwin walked beside the prince. The sound of the breathing grew louder in his ears. He knew instinctively that he should go on a few more doors. Then something inside made him jolt to a stop.

'Here,' he muttered, pointing to a door. 'He's in here.'

Auvlin took a deep breath and lifted up a latch. The door opened and he put his head through the gap, then looked back. 'Come in,' he mouthed.

Edwin went first after Auvlin, then Perpetua and Bellwin, all creeping in as silently as they could. They were in some sort of ante-chamber, with a small pain of thick glass in the door between them and the next room. It looked as if this entrance area was used for observation. And what they could see was quite a sight.

There were two men in the room. One was very well built and was sitting strapped to a chair, back facing them. He looked to be asleep as his head was resting on his obviously massive chest. Edwin watched it move: it synchronised perfectly with what he could hear in his head. 'That's him,' he said. 'The Enersh guy . . .'

The other man was standing to one side of him. He

held some kind of surgical instrument, and he dug it into what looked like a fresh wound on the man's shoulder. He cut something away and put it in a dish to one side.

'He's taking samples,' whispered Perpetua. 'Something to clone from, I bet.'

Directly opposite the bound man was an open metal door. The room on the other side was cast in shadow, but was just visible. On the inside of the door were three large bolts; it reminded Edwin of a prison.

'I think that room is where the man is kept,' Auvlin said. He looked at the others. 'Listen to me. I have a plan . . .'

A few minutes later, everyone nodded that they were ready. Perpetua whispered, 'One, two, three – go!' and Auvlin and Edwin burst through the door, followed quickly by the other two. The man only had time to turn and look before Auvlin jumped on his back, knocking the instrument from his hand. Edwin, Perpetua and Bellwin seized the back of the chair and began to push towards the open door. The man sitting in it was huge. He stirred and took a deep breath, and Edwin winced. The chair inched forward. They pushed again and it slid across the floor.

Edwin looked around. Auvlin was sitting on the top of the other man, doing his best to keep him down. 'Keep going!' he wailed.

There was an almighty heave and the chair scraped

through the door, toppling into the room with the man face down. Edwin, Perpetua and Bellwin bundled in behind it.

'We're in!' Perpetua cried. 'Auvlin, we're in!'

Auvlin scrambled to his feet. The man grabbed his ankle, but Auvlin spun around, kicked his hand away and raced for the door. He ran through and Edwin and Bellwin threw themselves against it. The door banged shut and they rushed to slam the bolts home.

BANG! BANG! BANG!

Everyone dropped to their knees, breathless. The man in the chair was stirring. The deep creases in his cheeks emphasised the savage expression. He opened his eyes for a few seconds.

'I'd better do this quickly,' Edwin gasped and he fumbled in his pocket for the sceptre. 'Bellwin,' he said, 'PLEASE get this noise out of my head!'

Bellwin waved his hand and the sound of the man's breathing disappeared. Edwin and Auvlin heaved the chair over. The man lay slumped to one side, but he opened his eyes again.

'He looks sedated,' Perpetua said. 'That's a bit of luck. Though he might be coming round . . .'

Edwin took out the relic's box and opened one of the man's hands. It was huge, almost twice the size of his. He opened the box, tipped the sceptre into the palm and bent the fingers over. Suddenly, the man seemed to wake up. He opened his hand. Edwin grimaced. 'You're gonna have to help me with this . . .'

Auvlin and Perpetua knelt beside Edwin and helped wrench the man's fingers over the sceptre. The man jolted, his forearms straining. His fingers were almost back open again.

'Tie his fist with something,' Perpetua cried. She loosened her belt with one hand then wrapped it around and around the man's fingers. She pulled it tight and he kicked out.

'Oh, no you don't,' she said under her breath.

'It's three minutes, right?' Edwin said, his fingers turning white.

'Yes,' Bellwin answered, peering through the circle of glass in the door. 'But we have another problem . . . Umbrian guards are here.'

There was the sound of heavy footsteps, followed by a pounding on the door. 'Open it,' someone growled. 'Or you die.'

Perpetua looked at Edwin. 'We didn't think about what would happen once we found him,' she said, her voice quivering.

'I know,' was all Edwin could say. He urged the seconds to tick by. He'd lost count ages ago . . . he had no idea how long they had to wait. 'When will we know it's worked?' he whined.

'I do not know,' Auvlin said. 'But we surely will, somehow.'

There was a sudden chanting from the other side of

the door. All the bolts began to slide back. Bellwin held out his hand. 'Astill!' he blurted. The bolts stopped. The chanting on the other side became quicker. 'Astill,' Bellwin repeated, again and again until there was barely a pause between each word.

The man on the floor bucked like a bull in a crate. His knee caught Perpetua and she was flung back against the wall. Edwin fumbled for the leather strap, pulled it, then felt Perpetua's hands on his. 'Hold on,' she said, 'just hold on . . .'

Edwin's arms were shaking. His biceps began to burn with pain. When would these three minutes end? He felt his face turn red. Auvlin was crouched in front, his fingers encasing the man's fist. He began to writhe from side to side. Come on, come on, Edwin urged silently . . . COME ON . . .

There was a high pitched whistle. The whistle turned into words. 'Birth . . . ninth day, second month, 25842,' it said mechanically. Death . . . third day, eighth month, Year 25897.'

Edwin looked at Auvlin. He still didn't get how the Hysterians worked out their years. 'Is that first date right . . . is he the one?'

Auvlin looked up, his face flushed. 'Yes,' he said. 'And the last day is . . . today.'

Edwin's throat clamped. 'Yes, yes, 'course it is,' he mumbled. 'We have to do it!' He looked up as the bolts once again began to slide back. Bellwin carried on chanting but tried to hold them with his hands. Auvlin took a knife out of his coat and held it against the man's chest.

'Quickly,' Bellwin wailed. 'They can almost opened the door.'

Auvlin set his jaw, clenched his fist around the hilt of the knife and slid it in. The man buckled, his chest expanding against the blade. Blood spurted onto Auvlin's hand, but he held steady. It pulsed out of the wound, gushing in sequence with the beat of a heart. The man stiffened, his arms pushed sideways and the bonds tying him to the chair broke. Auvlin was thrown over with the man, but still he held on. Edwin jumped beside him, closing his fingers over Auvlin's . They both pushed the knife down as hard as they could.

The door flew open. Guards rushed in and wrenched Auvlin and Edwin away from the man. He was still writhing on the floor, but his movements started to slow. Edwin and Auvlin stopped struggling and even the guards holding them were transfixed by the sight. The man's face was contorted with pain, his limbs shaking, his throat straining to take in air. Then, suddenly, he stopped moving. His mouth fell open and he let out a long, dry breath.

'He's dead!' Edwin said, sounding almost hysterical. 'We've killed him. We've killed him!'

But an Umbrian was kneeling on the floor, next to the body. He fumbled in his cloak for something, then held up a bright red stone.

'Spiritus Hereticus,' he wailed. 'Alliveria!'

Edwin heard Perpetua gasp. A shiver raced up his spine. The spirit of the revered Umbrian leader, Hereticus . . . put into the tall, strong body of a fearless fighter. Edwin whispered, 'The Umbrian original . . . the spirit had found a home . . .'

A thin metallic stream began to rush from the mouth of the man's body.

'Yes,' hissed the Umbrian. 'Yes . . .'

'It's the spirit of Hereticus! Edwin yelled. 'Someone do something!'

'Get my hand free,' Bellwin said. 'Get it free!'

The spirit was seeping towards the stone. Auvlin and Edwin tried to wrestle free from their guards. Edwin looked over. He wasn't far from Bellwin. He leaned against his guard, forcing the Umbrian backwards, then brought up his legs and kicked out as far as he could. His foot caught the left arm of Bellwin's guard and the wizard's hand was free.

The last of the metallic stream slunk out of the body towards the red stone. Bellwin pointed at it, took a breath and shouted, 'Terminas!'

At once a trail of purple smoke rushed to the tail of the spirit. There was a flash of bright light and the stone was knocked from the Umbrian's hand. It spun in the air, its deep glow pulsating. A piercing scream hit the walls. For a moment Edwin saw the image of a face, hollow and deathly, hanging in the air. The stone hit the floor and crumbled into dust. The kneeling Umbrian cried out and put his hands to his head. The guards looked at each other in silence.

'Bellwin,' Edwin asked shakily. 'Did it work?'

'Yes,' Bellwin whispered, his arms dropping to his sides. 'Yes . . .'

'Then we've killed the spirit of Hereticus too,' Edwin said. He let out a strangled laugh. 'We've killed him . . .'

'In the name of Janus,' Auvlin gasped, closing this eyes. 'Thank goodness.'

'Hysterian scum!'

A hand yanked Edwin by the collar and he was pulled up to face the Umbrian man. The man's skin was sallow and his angular face shone with a sheen of grease. His beady eyes bored into Edwin and he jerked his head towards Auvlin.

'I have seen him before,' he sneered. 'But who are you?'

'Edwin Spencer,' came the answer. 'And proud of it!'

The man wrenched Edwin up and dragged him over to the body. 'This is your doing – and you will die for it! Bring them all to their feet!' the Umbrian shouted, shoving Edwin to one side.

Edwin, Perpetua, Auvlin and Bellwin were all pulled up. Two guards each held their arms behind their backs.

'Experience shows us that the execution of Hysterians must be swift,' the Umbrian said. 'Too often we have delayed – often for our own pleasure – and seen our prisoners escape. So today I will try you, decide your sentence . . . and carry it out.'

'Who are you to decide our fate?' Auvlin shouted. 'No Umbrian is fit to try *any* Hysterian.'

The man walked towards Auvlin, his eyes glittering. 'I am the Umbrian Master Wizard,' he spat. 'But I doubt you recognise me . . .'

'You disgust me!' Auvlin roared. 'You are your people are incapable of living in peace. You want everything! You want *everything*!'

The Master Wizard smiled. 'Yes, we do,' he said. 'And we will get it.' He pulled a sword from his belt and held it above his head. 'The four accused are tried for the extermination of the spirit of our great leader, Hereticus. They are found guilty of this crime and are sentenced to death by beheading. The execution will be carried out by me, the Master Wizard, with all the pleasure and joy an act of aggression on a citizen of Hysteria can bring. Witnesses?'

Several voices answered, 'Yes, master.' The wizard lowered his sword and pointed it at Bellwin as he walked slowly forward. The guards behind Bellwin put him at arm's length. He stood shaking, watching the Master Wizard advance. Edwin's chin began to quiver. He heard Perpetua whimper. The Master Wizard began to lift his blade. Edwin scrunched up his eyes. Tears spilled onto his cheeks. This couldn't be happening . . .

dear, dear Bellwin. After all they'd done . . . after everything they'd saved.

Bellwin whispered, 'Goodbye . . .'

There was the swish of metal through air; a loud roar.

'DIE!'

Edwin jolted. Primus!

Edwin opened his eyes. The Master Wizard lay on the floor. A line of the King's Guard streamed into the room. Suddenly Edwin was being fought over. His arms were wrenched free. He heard groans and the Umbrian guards crumpled. Auvlin, Perpetua and Bellwin were also free. They stood there, dazed. Auvlin looked up and Edwin followed his gaze. King Janus stood in the doorway, his sword smeared red and his eyes glowering.

'What in the name of Hysteria are you doing?' he boomed. He strode into the room, his face set in anger.

Auvlin stepped forward. 'We have killed the spirit of Hereticus, father.'

'You have done *what*?' the king said. He looked as if he couldn't quite process what he'd just heard.

'It's true,' Edwin said. He pointed down. 'That man is the original of the Umbrian army clones – they made them *all* from him. We wanted to weaken their army and this seemed the best way.'

Janus looked at the body. He shook his head, but couldn't seem to find any words.

'What we *didn't* know,' said Perpetua, 'was that the

Umbrian wizards had put the spirit of Hereticus into him.'

'We killed the man,' Edwin said. 'Then their Master Wizard tried to take Hereticus's spirit out of it . . . but Bellwin killed that, too.'

'It is a good deed, father,' Auvlin said. He touched his father's arm. 'I am sorry we kept it secret from you.'

Janus looked at Auvlin and half-smiled. Finally, he spoke. 'I can think of no greater deed done in the name of our kingdom.' He looked back at the body. 'The evil of Hereticus within a body as strong as any man could be. There would have been no greater danger to Hysteria.'

Primus put the blade of his sword beneath the man's lifeless hand and lifted its fingers. 'This would have been our future. I do not know if we could have resisted it.' He looked at Edwin. 'You have done many things to help Hysteria, Edwin, but there is none more important than this.'

Edwin felt a lump come to his throat. He looked at Perpetua and smiled. She tried to smile back but her bottom lip was shaking.

'I know it was a bit mad to come here on our own. But it was worth it.' Edwin looked at the king. 'And I'd do it all again.'

Auvlin put his arm around Edwin's shoulders. 'Me also,' he whispered. 'And it would be an honour.'

Two soldiers suddenly appeared at the door. 'The villa is secure, Lord Primus. We may walk around it freely.'

'How many men did you bring, Your Majesty?' Edwin asked.

'Five hundred,' Janus replied. He smiled. 'We did not know what we would find.' He slid his blood-stained sword into its sheath. 'I need to breathe fresh air. Come outside with me. We will talk in the morning light of Umbria.'

Perpetua, Bellwin and Auvlin followed Janus straight away. But something made Edwin hang back. He'd spotted the Sceptre of Jozeponi behind the Umbrian wizard's body. This was Ahven's. It should really go back to Janus. He bent down to pick it up, but hesitated. Now he knew what the spirit had been trying to tell him, would it still appear?

'Edwin!' Perpetua called.

He snatched up the relic and closed his fingers. It felt cold – just like any metal. Edwin smiled; maybe the spirit was now at peace. 'Edwin, come on! I was just telling Janus how powerful the man was . . .'

For the next few minutes Perpetua did nothing but instruct Edwin as to his next move. As they walked up the stairs and along passages, he barely registered the King's Guard milling around the villa. His head suddenly felt very light and he was glad to feel a cool breeze as they emerged into the morning air.

Janus came to a stop and they all gathered around him. 'Now,' he said. 'I want you to tell me everything from the start.'

Perpetua took a deep breath. 'Well—'

But there was a sudden high-pitched whistle. Everyone looked at Edwin. He himself looked down. 'Birth,' a metallic voice began, '. . . twenty-second day, first month, year 25,871 . . .' Edwin opened his hand; the sceptre was glowing yellow. 'Death . . . twenty-third day, fifth month, year 26,004 . . .'

Edwin looked at Perpetua. She didn't seem to understand the dates either.

Auvlin's face had drained white. He took a step to Edwin, his expression uncertain. 'The date it has given you,' he said slowly. 'It is your birth date . . .'

Edwin swallowed. 'I suppose it must be, in *Hysterian* years. But I don't understand how to work it out.'

Auvlin's lips began to tremble. He reached out and touched Edwin's arm. His fingers were shaking. 'I understand *this*,' he whispered. 'That is my birth date too, Edwin.'

Edwin blinked and repeated Auvlin's words in his head. He tried to process what Auvlin was saying. 'But how can it be . . . you're older than me. They aged me by two years to take your place . . .'

But then Edwin remembered something. He looked at Perpetua – it was obvious she had thought of it, too. Time in Hysteria moved faster than on Earth. He would have always been growing at a slower pace. Of course. It all fitted . . .

Edwin felt everything go into slow motion. He

couldn't focus properly. He couldn't speak. He felt Auvlin clutch his arm tight.

'That is my birth date, too,' Auvlin repeated. 'You look exactly like me. There can be no other answer – we are brothers, Edwin. We are *twin brothers*.'

The next thing Edwin knew Janus was holding him and Auvlin in his arms, his chest shuddering. 'Auvlin, are you sure?'

'Yes, father,' said Auvlin shakily. 'It is the purpose of the sceptre – to give the date of death and birth.' Janus tightened his grip.

'This was my dearest wish,' he said. 'How can it have come true?'

'I don't understand,' Edwin said, burying his face in the king's hair. 'I don't understand . . .'

Edwin was confused. He was in shock. But . . . but he was *happy*. This man, who he loved more than anyone else, the man who he wanted to be his father . . . *was* his father. He couldn't take it in. He couldn't let himself believe it was true. But it explained so much. Edwin felt as if his heart would burst.

'I want to believe it, Your Majesty,' Edwin croaked. 'I want to be your son.'

Janus loosened his grip and Edwin was able to look up into his eyes. Their deep blue shone with tears; it was the most beautiful sight Edwin had ever seen.

'Do not call me Your Majesty, my boy,' Janus said softly. 'Call me father.'

Chapter Fifteen

For Edwin, the journey back to Emporium Castle was done in a daze. Everything had changed. He wasn't an earthling, he was a royal of Hysteria. He wasn't born in London, he was born in Jozeponi. Mr and Mrs Spencer were not his parents. Katie, Jenny and Ollie weren't his siblings. No wonder he'd never fitted in.

It was Perpetua who remembered to explain the story behind the seven skeletons. Janus was very relieved to hear that this mystery had also been solved, but he was amazed that even the Umbrians could bring themselves to farm humans for blood.

No one could remember the exact year the sceptre had given for Edwin's death. Auvlin was sure it was

26,000 and something, which meant Edwin would have a very long life. That was good enough for him. He just wanted to get on and enjoy living it.

Edwin kept glancing over at Janus and Auvlin as they rode through the day and into the night. These men were his family. Deep down, had he known that?

'Are you OK?' Perpetua asked Edwin for the hundredth time, as their horses plodded up the winding paths towards the castle gates.

'Yeah,' Edwin answered again. 'It just feels a bit, you know, a bit strange . . .'

'Gosh,' Perpetua said. 'I've been friends with you for two or three years and all the time you were an alien. If I'd have known, I could have reported you to the authorities – they might have taken you for experiments.'

Edwin smiled. 'That's all a bit Doctor Who,' he said. 'I think I've got the same bits and pieces as everyone else on Earth.'

'But you're royalty, too,' Perpetua sighed. 'Who would have thought that a prince could be so bad at his lessons?'

The night watchman opened the castle gates and everyone rode through followed by the King's Guard. Ollwin, Lorius and Mersium rushed out to meet them in the inner courtyard.

'What has happened, Janus?' Mersium asked quickly.

'We have brought all four back without loss,' Janus replied. 'And they have done two great things for

Hysteria. First, they found the original of the Umbrian's fearless and savage soldier clones and killed him. Umbria will never again be able to raise an army of such ferocity.' He smiled. 'And in the process, and even better, they have destroyed the spirit of Hereticus. They could have done Hysteria no better service.'

Of course it took more than a few minutes to explain exactly how all this had been done, but afterwards even Lorius sounded slightly impressed. 'An ill-advised trip,' he said coldly. 'But a worthy outcome. We have you to thank again, Spencer.'

'Yes, well done, Edwin,' Ollwin said, shaking his hand. 'Well done . . .'

Janus looked at Edwin and put his hand on his shoulder. 'Something else has come to light. Something wonderful, something that could only be dreamed of. It will bring joy to Auvlin and to me – joy to all of us – joy to all of Hysteria.'

'Yes?' Ollwin said excitedly. 'What is it, Your Majesty?'

Auvlin moved to stand beside Edwin, and the king smiled. 'Two princes of the Janus line return to Emporium castle this night, my dear friends.'

Lorius frowned. 'What do you mean, Sire?'

'I mean that in future you will need to address Edwin with a little more respect, Lorius. Edwin Spencer is not of Earth . . . is not of another breed. He is Auvlin's brother; my son. I have proof – there is no doubt.'

Ollwin whimpered and fell to his knees. Mersium

gave a cry and hugged Janus and then both boys. Lorius stood there, staring.

'I do not know what to say,' he muttered, looking down. 'I . . .'

'You don't need to say anything,' Edwin said. He offered Lorius his hand. 'Friends?'

Lorius looked up, then into Edwin's eyes. 'Friends,' he repeated. They shook hands and Edwin was sure that, just for a moment, Lorius's skin was warm.

Ollwin got to his feet. 'I always knew there was something else about you, Edwin,' he said joyfully. He nearly bowled him over with a hug, but suddenly jumped back. 'Sire,' he said, looking at Janus. 'We have a visitor. It is the physician from Jozeponi – the man you have been trying to find.'

Janus's eyes lit up. 'Do you know if he is able to help us?'

'There's loads more stuff we need to ask him now,' Edwin added.

'We have told him nothing,' Mersium replied. 'We decided to wait for your return.'

'Then I will see him straight away,' Janus said eagerly. 'Has Brolin continued to treat Georgiara?'

'Yes,' Ollwin replied. 'She is making great progress.'

Janus walked towards the door. 'Then perhaps she can join us. This could be the hour that we learn everything . . .'

Everyone followed the king to the Throne Room, where Georgiara and Brolin were brought to meet them. Janus looked really very pleased to see her and Edwin and Perpetua couldn't believe how different she looked from only a few days ago. She told Janus that she now knew who he was and that he had been married to her cousin. She knew Ahven had died, but she couldn't remember how. The king patted her hand and advised her to sit down. Brolin took his place behind her.

Auvlin and Edwin stood next to their father as he took his place on the throne. Perpetua looked up at them admiringly.

The physician from Jozeponi was escorted in and Janus bowed his head as the man presented himself.

'King Janus – I am Atolinus of Jozeponi.'

'I have been looking for you,' Janus replied.

'Yes,' Atolinus looked down. 'For many years I expected you to come for me. I did not think it would take this long . . .'

Janus swallowed. 'Do you know what happened to my wife, Atolinus?'

'Yes, Sire.'

'And you know why I was told that she had given birth to only one child?'

'Yes.'

Georgiara suddenly raised her hand. 'I think I have

met your before, sir,' she said to Atolinus. 'Do you know my face?'

Atolinus smiled. 'Yes, my lady. I treated your family many times.'

Georgiara put her hand to her mouth. 'I remember,' she said slowly. 'I realised yesterday that both my father and mother were dead. They died within weeks of each other, only months after my cousin. I remember you at their house . . . you were kind to us all.'

Atolinus bowed his head. 'Thank you, Georgiara.'

Janus turned to her. 'Other memories may come back to you here,' he said gently. 'Be brave, my dear.'

Edwin glanced at Perpetua and she smiled. He needed her right now. He was about to find out how he was born . . . how he got to Earth . . . and why he was taken there.

Janus nodded at Atolinus. 'We will hear your story. Please begin.'

Atolinus composed himself. 'Queen Ahven and Georgiara saw each other a great deal throughout her pregnancy and on a few occasions I attended the queen at the house in Jozeponi.' He thought for a second. 'On one such occasion a woman had been to see Ahven before me. She was a fortune teller and after she left Ahven and Georgiara were very upset.'

'Why?' Janus snapped. 'What had the woman told her?'

'She had told Queen Ahven that she was carrying

twin boys. Ahven did not ask about her own fate, but asked about that of her sons.'

'And what was the answer?' Auvlin said, taking one step down from the throne.

'The woman said that a reading before birth was difficult, that it was only possible to foresee one or two major events in future life. But what she *did* see was not good fortune.' Atolinus took a deep breath. 'She foresaw that one of the princes would be attacked in Hysteria his fourteenth or fifteenth year with a dagger. But she could not tell Ahven which son – and it was unclear whether the boy would live or die. It seemed that he would be in a half-life.'

Edwin's mouth fell open. He looked at Auvlin. 'She was talking about when Hercula stabbed you . . . when you were lying in the mausoleum.'

Janus stood up. 'So what decision did my wife take?'

'I remember!' Georgiara leapt to her feet. Her legs buckled and she crumpled to the floor. Janus rushed to her and propped her up. She gradually came to, opening her eyes wide. 'I remember!' she repeated.

'Hush, Georgiara,' Janus said gently, stroking her hair. 'There is no need for this now . . . Atolinus will tell us everything.'

'No, Your Majesty,' said Georgiara, sitting up unsteadily. 'I will help. It is my duty.'

Janus nodded and sat beside Georgiara on the floor. 'We spoke at length, Ahven and me,' Georgiara began.

'She was desperately worried. Which of her sons would be exposed to such violence?' She shook her head. 'There was no way of knowing The woman had told Ahven *when* her babies would be born, so she decided to come here and send one away as soon as they arrived. The spirit guide had told her of the other world, and Ahven thought that he would perhaps be safe from the prophecy there. Of course she did not know if she was parting with the right baby . . . but she could not bear to lose both.'

Janus put a hand to his head. 'Oh, Ahven,' he sighed. 'Why did you not tell me?'

Georgiara took the king's hand. 'Her plan was that if the child she kept had not been attacked by the age of sixteen, she would tell you about his twin and he would be sent for. She entrusted this secret to me, so that if she died before the twins' sixteenth birthday, I would tell you in her place.'

'So my mother did not know that when she was going to die?' Auvlin said. 'She did not know when she went to Jozeponi?'

'No, Prince Auvlin,' Atolinus said.

Janus frowned. 'But how could Ahven *not* know her fate – the relic that she owned gave the date of birth *and* death . . .'

'It does indeed,' Brolin said briskly. 'It does indeed.'

'Our grandmother Leana gave Ahven the relic to act as a host for her spirit guide,' Georgiara said. 'It was when she was eighteen, long before she was even married. Leana told Ahven what else it is was for, but Ahven did not want to know when she would die. She kept it purely for contact with the spirit world.'

Janus smiled and Georgiara took his hand. She then looked at Edwin. 'When you were born, I wrapped you in a blanket, and she held you close. She kissed you very tenderly and stroked your face . . . she said that one day she would come back for you and that your mother and father loved you very much.'

Edwin felt a lump in his throat. He swallowed against it, but wasn't able to stop tears trickling down his cheeks.

'Then I took you from her. Her eyes followed you until I left the room and she whispered goodbye. I travelled with a wizard from Jozeponi to Emporium Castle. We were smuggled in by a maid and together we travelled through the vortex to Earth. We found a family for you – one that I hoped would look after you until you came back to Hysteria. One that I thought would love you.'

Edwin closed his eyes. His mother loved him . . . he knew she did. But she wasn't the woman who had brought him to life, who had helped him take his very first breath. Edwin sank to his knees and sobbed. Auvlin and Perpetua ran to him. They put their arms around him. They cried for his sadness. They cried for his happiness.

'Ahven gave me the relic,' Georgiara carried on. 'She asked me to leave it with her baby son as a keepsake of his Hysterian heritage. To her, the relic was a very precious thing . . . she gave it to Edwin as a symbol of how precious he was, and how heartbroken she was to send him away. And then Ahven became ill. . .' Georgiara's voice began to break. 'She died and I was left alone with her secret. Then my mother and father passed away so quickly, one after the other, and I became so, so confused . . .''

Edwin, Perpetua and Auvlin stood up. Edwin wiped his face with his sleeve. 'So, my mum – my mother on Earth – found the relic in my cot. She thought it was a present someone had left for me.' He sniffed. 'And it kind of was, wasn't it?'

Perpetua rubbed her eyes and cleared her throat. 'You know what all this means,' she said.

Edwin looked at her. 'What?'

'That the real son of Mr and Mrs Spencer is somewhere else.'

'I am afraid that is not so,' Georgiara said.

'Eh?' Edwin said. 'How come? You must have swapped me for another boy.'

'We did,' Georgiara replied. 'But first I used the relic to see if any of the babies would not have long to live. There was one . . . he looked healthy, but it seemed he would die within a day.' She smiled sadly. 'He was a similar size to you and his hair was the same colour.

The only real difference was the eyes.'

'OH MY GOD!' Perpetua screeched. 'Edwin – you once told me that the day after you were born, your mum thought there was something different about your eyes. She was right!'

Edwin had to think for a second. All of this was almost too much to take in. 'She *also* said she didn't know what to call me and suddenly *Edwin* popped into her head.' He looked at Janus. 'It sounds sort of Hysterian, don't you think?'

Janus got up and walked to Edwin. He put his hands on his shoulders. 'I thought that the very first time I heard your name,' he said. 'Perhaps the relic had some other powers – powers of influence?'

'What happened to the other baby?' Perpetua said sadly.

'I stayed on earth until he died and I cared for him,' Georgiara whispered. 'He was in no pain. For the day that he lived, he was loved.'

'Poor thing,' Perpetua croaked. Edwin reached out and held her hand.

Janus sat back on his throne. 'A man and woman on Earth lost a son, but they did not know.' He looked at Edwin. 'My boy, are you going to stay with us?'

Edwin felt his stomach twinge. He'd been so excited about being Janus's son, he hadn't thought about his life on Earth. If he didn't go back his mother and father, Mr and Mrs Spencer, would never see their third child again. 'I want to stay here,' Edwin murmured. 'But what will it do to them? They'll never know what's happened to me . . .'

The king smiled sadly. 'You are a remarkable young man,' he said softly. 'I knew very soon after I met you that you were loyal and unselfish, but now I know how very much.'

'Do *you* want me to stay, Your Majesty?'

Janus had to pause for quite a while before he answered. 'The day Auvlin was born was a bittersweet one. I had a child to love, I had a son, I had an heir to my throne. But I knew my wife was so ill that she might die. *This* day reminds me very much of then – I find I have another child to love, another son, another heir. But I know that he may not be able to remain by my side.' Janus swallowed. 'Yes, Edwin, of course I want you to stay.'

Edwin held Janus's gaze and he couldn't hold back another flow of tears. He looked around. Everyone looked hopeful; they didn't want Edwin to go back to Earth either.

That was, everyone except Perpetua. Edwin descended the steps and stood in front of her. He took both her hands, and watched her bottom lip tremble. 'What should I do, Einstein?'

'Oh, you don't need to be a genius to work that one out,' she croaked. 'Think about what you have here – you're a prince, Edwin. People love you, people respect you, people want to be around you. You've saved Hysteria, competed for Hysteria, changed Hysteria's history for the better. Here, in this country, in this castle, with this family, you are good at *so very much.*'

Edwin sighed and squeezed her fingers. 'It's a bit of a no-brainer,' he said.

Perpetua coughed and glanced around. 'That means it's a question that doesn't require any thought.' She looked back at Edwin and smiled. 'Maybe you *should* think about it . . . but my guess is you already know the answer.'

CHAPTER SIXTEEN

PERPETUA STAYED ON IN HYSTERIA for a few weeks after everything had settled down. She kept saying 'Oh, I'll go home in one or two days', but one or two days came and went several times and she was still there in Emporium Castle. Edwin was just starting to wonder if she would *ever* go back to Earth, when she suddenly announced she wanted to go home that very day.

'Oh. That's a bit sudden,' Edwin said. 'Have you left something in the oven?'

Of course Perpetua pointed out that even if she *had*, time was going to be reversed again and any burnt offerings would be recovered. 'And anyway,' she said, 'I'm far too busy to cook.' She crossed her arms. 'And I hate it.' She unfolded her arms and blinked. 'And, *actually*, I'm not very good at it.'

'Blimey,' Edwin muttered. 'Do your parents know?'

'Not yet.' She smiled. 'They still think I'm perfect!'

Everything was prepared for Perpetua's return home and all the court gathered to see her off. Apart from Edwin, she left the king until last.

'Dear Perpetua,' Janus said, hugging her tight. 'You have played no small part in the saving of Hysteria. We owe you so much.'

'I've loved it,' she croaked. 'I've loved every single minute of it. I wouldn't change a thing.'

'I am glad. Will you come back to see us? The vortex will always be there.'

Perpetua looked up. 'You mean I can visit?' She frowned. 'I don't know if I should. What if something went wrong?'

'It is your decision. But whatever happens, I wish you well.'

Perpetua gave Bellwin one last hug, then walked to the vortex with Edwin. They stood facing each other and for a few minutes they still couldn't find any words.

'I can't believe I'm going home without you,' Perpetua said eventually, her voice quivering.

'Me neither,' Edwin said shakily. 'I'm . . . I'm gonna miss you.'

Perpetua forced a smile. 'Of course you won't!' she laughed. 'The minute I've gone you'll be whisked off to a banquet, taken for sword-fighting practice or be riding out with Mersium to the crystal mines.'

'Maybe,' Edwin replied. 'But I'll *still* miss you.'

'Oh, Edwin . . .' Perpetua leapt into Edwin's arms. She sobbed and cried and left a watery mark on his tunic, but finally said she had to go.

'You'll always be my friend, Edwin Spencer,' she whispered. 'And that makes me very proud.'

Edwin couldn't say any more. He could only nod and squeeze Perpetua's hand before she walked into the vortex. And when she'd gone, when she'd disappeared into the warm orange haze, he remembered he hadn't asked if he'd ever see her again.

EPILOGUE

Templeton Grove Comprehensive School
Stinching Lane, London N34 4BO
Head teacher: Mr I. M. Smellings

Dr & Dr M Allbright
127 Swottingham Road
Templeton Grove
London N34 5BA

22 July

Dear Dr and Dr Allbright

I promised I would write to you at the end of the school year regarding our concerns about Perpetua. As we had all observed, Perpetua seemed to suffer a great degree of unhappiness following the mysterious disappearance of

Edwin Spencer. However, she has continued the sudden recovery she began around Easter and although her school work had never suffered she has rediscovered her enthusiasm. As you know, in the last few months she has produced some astonishing theories regarding space and time and has brought to school some very interesting specimens of rock. Indeed, Perpetua now seems to be in robust health, taking completely in her stride the increased episodes of 'mass déjà vu' that everyone has been experiencing.

With all good wishes for the summer holiday.

I M Smellings

ABOUT THE AUTHOR

J. D. IRWIN (who also answers to Julie) started writing *Edwin Spencer Mission Improbable*, the first book to feature Edwin and Perpetua in 2001 when pregnant with her daughter. She'd been writing grown-up fiction on and off for many years, but maternity leave gave her a chance to have a serious stab at something else. She soon discovered that writing stories for children was much more fun, and from then on didn't want to write anything else!

www.jdirwin.com

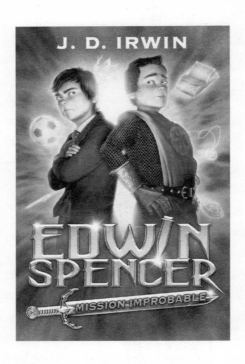

'Calling Master Edwin Spencer! You are summoned
by the court of King Janus of Hysteria. Pass
through that vortex that appears before you!'

Edwin Spencer has enough problems at school as
it is, without strange voices calling him into another
dimension! But when he is sucked into the peculiar
kingdom of Hysteria on a secret mission he feels very
at home. This could be his chance at last to be a hero,
even if he does have Perpetua Allbright, school swot, as
his sidekick.

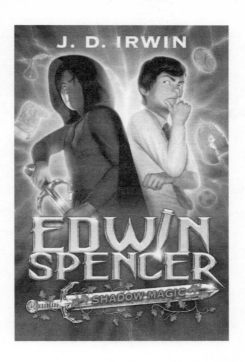

'I've got to hurtle through a tunnel of fire into another blimmin' parallel. All because Auvlin doesn't want to look like a loser?!'

When Edwin Spencer is summoned back through the vortex to help Prince Auvlin during a tournament, he's more that a little suspicious. Once in Hysteria things aren't as they seem. Why is Auvlin acting all weird? Who are those strange riders in the forest? And how come no one seems to notice Perpetua, the most irritating sidekick that ever existed?

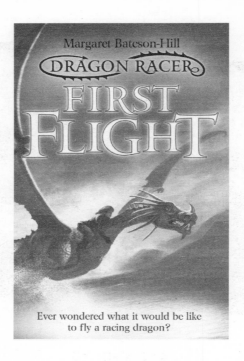

Margaret Bateson-Hill

DRAGON RACER

FIRST FLIGHT

Ever wondered what it would be like
to fly a racing dragon?

*The dragon's face was so close Joanna could feel its hot
breath on her cheeks. She reached up to touch it . . .*

Joanna Morris has no idea that her life is about to change
as she shoots to stardom as the youngest dragon flyer in
the country. Flying the stunning silver spiked-back racing
dragon, Excelsior, is more exciting than anything she's
ever known and he's soon her closest friend in the world.

But beneath the glitz and glamour of dragon racing lie
burning ambitions that threaten to consume anyone that
stands in the way – including the sport's rising stars . . . .

WELCOME TO
SCREAMING SANDS
the ghastliest ghost town in the world!

Middle Spit Sands is a dull, rainy seaside town, until Davey puts an advert in a mysterious newspaper to attract customers to his parents' ice cream café. Soon some seriously spooky guests start arriving and Screaming Sands, seaside ghost town, is born.

In this **screamingly** funny new series, you'll find zombie donkeys, blankets that attack and undead weddings – just another ordinary day in Screaming Sands.

You can find out more about J. D. Irwin
and other Catnip books by visiting
www.catnippublishing.co.uk